CARNIVORES

J. R. LEVITT

W9-BSU-413

A SIGNET BOOK

Signet
Published by the Penguin Group
Penguin Books USA Inc., 375 Hudson Street,
New York, New York 10014, U.S.A.
Penguin Books Ltd, 27 Wrights Lane
London W8 5TZ, England
Penguin Books Australia Ltd, Ringwood,
Victoria, Australia
Penguin Books Canada Ltd, 2801 John Street,
Markham, Ontario, Canada L3R 1B4
Penguin Books (N.Z.) Ltd, 182-190 Wairau Road,
Auckland 10, New Zealand

Penguin Books Ltd, Registered Offices:
Harmondsworth, Middlesex, England

Published by Signet, an imprint of New American Library, a di-
vision of Penguin Books USA Inc. This is an authorized reprint
of a hardcover edition published by St. Martin's Press.

First Signet Printing, December, 1990
10 9 8 7 6 5 4 3 2 1

Ⓢ   REGISTERED TRADEMARK—MARCA REGISTRADA

Printed in the United States of America

PUBLISHER'S NOTE
This is a work of fiction. Names, characters, places, and incidents either are the product of the author's imagination or are
used fictitiously, and any resemblance to actual persons, living
or dead, events, or locales is entirely coincidental.

ONE

You never really get used to dead people. Oh, I suppose you do if you work at the morgue, but that's a different thing. The ceiling fluorescents hummed quietly, throwing a cold light on the figure lying in the corner of the room. The woman on the stainless steel table had been attractive, and except for the fact that now the back of her head was caved in, she still was. Having been there only a couple of hours, she hadn't yet lost her individuality—she still seemed more like a person than a thing. She couldn't have been much older than seventeen. She had dark hair and was Mexican or Indian, very young and very pretty. Of course she was dead, and that kind of detracted from her appearance.

There was a ring on the third finger of her

left hand. I wondered if her husband knew yet. Probably not, unless he was the one who had killed her. Now that she was in the morgue it wasn't so bad; people in the morgue are supposed to be dead. It's when you find them stretched out in their living rooms that it gets to you a little.

Susan Lawson, an official nurse for the City and County of Salt Lake, came in to draw a blood sample from the dead girl. It would be sent to the state lab to be checked for drugs or alcohol. I needed to witness it and sign the forms, in case it went to court someday.

"How are things, Jason?" she asked, pulling back the sheet that was covering the girl's torso. "They been keeping you busy?"

"Always. Same old stuff."

"Just think of it as job security. That's what I do." She pulled the girl into a semisitting position, bracing her up with one hand while in the other she grasped a large-gauge needle attached to a syringe. Underneath the sheet the girl was naked, and as she was propped up her breasts sagged forward, swaying slightly from side to side. It was the ultimate vulnerability, the final invasion of privacy. Two hours ago, swelling with life, those breasts would have been the object of my avid interest. Now it made me feel uncomfortable even to look at them.

Nurse Susan got a good grip on the girl and rammed the needle into the middle of her chest. A couple of hours after death, the only place you can find blood that hasn't congealed yet is directly in the heart. It took a lot of pressure to get the needle in, and the trapped gasses in the lungs escaped through the girl's mouth with a sighing moan, protesting this final indignity. Susan started filling the syringe, taking no notice.

"Jesus," I said. "doesn't it ever bother you? I mean, when they're so young?"

"What, this?" Susan gave me a friendly smile. "Nope, not a bit. Dead is dead. To me, this is nothing more than a chunk of meat lying here."

"That's supposed to be my line. I'm the homicide cop."

"Oh, sure. Jason Coulter, man of stone. No feelings, no emotions." She gave a snort of disgust. "All you cops are the same. Whenever it's a young girl, especially if she's pretty, you sit there and shake your heads sadly and sigh. What difference does it make how old they were? Old or young, they're just as dead."

"Yeah, but still . . ."

"But still, nothing. Dead is dead."

Susan finished drawing the blood and released the girl, who flopped back down on the table. Somehow she looked more dead now. Susan threw away the needle, put the rest of the syringe in an evidence envelope, gave it to me to initial, put it in her bag, and was out the door in less than a minute.

"Gotta run," she called cheerfully over her shoulder. "There's a body from an auto-ped waiting for me over at St. Mark's, a kid hit by a delivery van."

An hour later I was back at the office, on the eighth floor of the Metro Building. Mike Volter, the homicide sergeant, was sitting at his desk filling out weekly time sheets. He looked up from his paperwork as I came in.

"What's the verdict, Jason? Accident or homicide?"

"I'd say homicide. She hit her head on the corner of a fireplace mantel. I can't see how there could be that much damage to the skull if she just took a tumble, so my guess would be that someone grabbed her by the hair and slammed her into it, probably more than once. We'll just have to wait for the autopsy. Or I could go back down and dust her face for prints."

Volter looked at me sideways. Mike was a very good cop, and not a bad sergeant, but he had no sense of humor whatsoever. I always believed that you needed a sense of humor to survive as a homicide dick, but he seemed to get along quite well without one. He let my remark pass without comment.

Mike had never known quite what to make of me, anyway. I wasn't his idea of a cop. He wore his hair short as a marine, which he used to be, and didn't understand any cop who didn't. He was by the book, 100 percent. I had been known to cut some corners in my time. I'd been with the department for quite a few years now, but in his eyes I was still just a little suspect as a police officer.

It didn't help any that I had been charged with assault my first year on the department, either. It really wasn't my fault. The guy had no business showing up in Salt Lake City, much less at my house.

Weasel Vance was his name. He was a couple of years older than me, the neighborhood bully where I grew up. He stole the brand-new Schwinn I had saved up all year for, trashed it, and dumped it back in my yard. Then he beat the crap out of me when I was foolish enough to take a swing at him one day.

He moved away, and I hadn't seen or thought about him until he showed up on my doorstep to install the cable for my TV. He had a good-sized beer belly and was losing his hair, but I knew him instantly. "Weasel?" I said in amazement, and he gaped at me. I didn't even think. I hit him with a left hook that spread his nose over his face.

Of course, it wasn't actually Weasel at all. It was some poor Mormon with six kids working a second job as a cable installer to make ends meet. I was lucky. I explained the whole thing, paid his doctor bills, bought his wife a new washing machine, and he dropped the charges. That saved me my job. That and the fact that Volter was smart enough to realize that I cleared a good many cases that the others couldn't or didn't. That guy sure did look like Weasel, though.

Now Volter settled his big frame farther back into his chair, the surplus roll of flesh around his middle straining across his belt. He looked up at me and said, "I'm going to reassign the case to Becker." He stopped and waited for my reaction. Becker was not one of my favorite people.

I shrugged. "You're the sergeant."

"Yeah, I know. I wish you'd try and remember that more often, Jason. The thing is, I've got something else I need you to concentrate on, you and Dave Warren. The Gilson case."

"Terrific. Great idea, Mike."

I turned away and walked over to the window. This was just what I needed, to work full time on a case there wasn't a chance in hell of solving. Sandra Gilson had been a waitress at the Kelly Green Lounge, over on Eighth South and State. One fine June day about a month ago, Sandra didn't show up for work. She hadn't been seen since. Her car was in the parking lot next to the lounge, locked up. About a week later a citizen called up and said he wanted to report something suspicious. He wouldn't give his name. He had been driving by the Kelly at about two A.M. on Friday, the last day anyone had seen Sandra, when he saw three men in the parking lot struggling with a young woman. He figured it was just a bunch of drunks and kept on driving. He couldn't get it out of his mind, though, and finally got a bad enough case of the guilts to call in and report it.

That was when the case was reassigned from Missing Persons to Homicide. The caller hadn't been able to give much of a description of the men, except that one of them was big and real fat. There were only two vehicles left in the lot that late at night. One of them was the Gilson girl's car. The other was a dark-colored pickup. All I had to do was to find a dark-colored pickup with an overweight driver. Or passenger. Nothing to it. I sighed at the thought.

"Why the sudden interest?" I asked. "Something new come up?"

Mike gestured at me with a pile of reports he held in his hand. "In the past nine months eight women have vanished in this valley. Not runaways. Women who were going to the store for a pack of cigarettes, women who disappeared on their way to work. One lady who was meeting her girlfriend for a double date. In three of those cases there was apparently a dark blue or green pickup seen in the area where the women disappeared."

I pulled a chair over to Mike's desk and slouched down. This put a whole different slant on things. This could be something very nasty.

"Serial killer?"

"Or killers. Three of them with the Gilson woman. I don't have to tell you how quiet I want this kept. If it gets out, it'll be a mess. And we don't even have any proof yet anyone's dead."

"They're dead."

"Yeah, but not officially. They're not dead until somebody finds the bodies."

"Any chance it's coincidence?"

Mike looked at me as if I were a retarded child. "Take a look at this," he said, throwing a sheaf of papers on the desk. "Just came in from county homicide."

It was a postmortem report from the medical examiner.

External Examination

The body is that of a well-developed, well-nourished Caucasian female. The body appears the stated age of twenty-five years. The body measures 1.64 m and weighs 49.8 kg. Rigor is fully developed. Lividity is posterior. The scalp hair is long and blond. The irises are light green. The mouth contains natural teeth.

The neck is symmetrical, and the chest has normal contours. The breasts are small. The abdomen is flat. The external genitalia are normal female. The extremities are symmetrical.

Clothing: The clothing consists of a leather jacket, shirt, brassiere, blue jeans, panties, red socks, and brown shoes.

Evidence of Injury

There is an 11-mm round gunshot wound of the right malar eminence located 8 cm in front of and 3 cm below the right external auditory meatus. The direction of the wound is right to left and slightly upward, perforating the right malar eminence, the right sphenoid bone, the brain stem at the level of the pons, and the inferior aspect of the left cerebellar hemisphere. There is a fracture defect of the left occipital bone, and a slightly deformed copper-jacketed approximately .38-caliber bullet is recovered in the occipital scalp at a point 3 cm behind and 1 cm below the left external auditory meatus.

She had been shot in the face, through the cheekbone, the bullet lodging on the opposite side of her head. I skimmed through the rest of the report. Various cuts, abrasions, and bruises. Evidence of genital and anal trauma. I thumbed through to the last page.

Opinion

It is my opinion Cynthia M. Stone, a twenty-five-year-old Caucasian female, died of a penetrating gunshot wound of the head.

Manner of death: Homicide.

"She disappeared the day before yesterday," Mike said. "They found her yesterday in a ditch out by Kennicott Copper. There were a bunch of tire tracks, nothing clear enough for a cast, but they look like they belong to a pickup truck."

"Same people?"

"You tell me."

I considered it briefly. "So I guess we'd better look into it. You talk to Dave about this yet?"

"Right before you came in. He just left for the day."

"Smart man. What did he say?"

"He seemed about as thrilled about it as you do."

"This is a hell of a thing to drop in our laps, Mike."

"If I didn't think—"

"Yeah, yeah. If you didn't think we could handle it, so on and so forth. Don't bullshit a bullshitter." I looked up at the clock. "It's past five. I'm going home, too."

"I want you guys on this tomorrow morning. First thing."

I waved an acknowledgment as I walked out the door.

On the way home I thought it over. It's always nice to get assigned the major cases, the big ones. It means that whatever they say, when crunch times comes, they know who can do the job. This one was going to be no prize, though. It's great to work an important case, but not one where you work for a year and still come up empty. That's what usually happens with serial killers. They're the toughest cases you can find.

Even the worst street scum rarely kill, and when they do, they usually get caught. But those who start killing for sexual motivations are a different animal altogether. They kill not once, but again and again. They become progressively bolder. The time intervals between killings grow shorter, and the murders themselves become increasingly more violent and grotesque. Some of them eventually lose control, become careless, and finally do get caught. But not all of them, by any means. Some are able to keep their sickness at least partway in check, and they manage to play out their nasty games for a long, long time. They never stop. They just go on and on, monsters dressed up like human beings, night vampires carrying misery and terror and death.

These were not pleasant thoughts, so as soon as I got home, I stopped thinking about it. I threw my coat on a chair and fixed myself a gin and tonic. It was hot out. There was a bunch of mail in the mailbox, just bills and junk. Two of them started out "Dear Homeowner," which let me off the hook right away. Another was a computer salutation. "Dear Mr. Coulter," was accurate enough, but then it went on to tell me about the special deals I could get now that I was past sixty-five.

I went into the kitchen to see what there was to eat, and the sound of the refrigerator door opening brought Stony in from the backyard on a dead run. Stony Lonesome, the resident feline, had moved into the house about seven years ago. I opened my front door one day and there he was, sitting on top of my car. I had never seen him before. The minute he saw the door open, he let out a yowl, jumped down, and ran past my feet into the kitchen, where he stalked around, tail waving, demanding something to eat. I was so bemused by his behavior that I gave him a can of tuna, and that was it. He settled right in and never left.

I opened a can of some horrible-looking stuff for him and was scraping it onto a paper plate when the phone rang. Dave Warren, my new and obviously reluctant partner, was on the line, and he was not happy.

"Jason. You heard?"

"I heard."

"Jesus. Why us?"

"Because Mike Volter has complete and total confidence—"

"Right. Sorry I asked. This is total bullshit. We're going to spend the next six months chasing ghosts. Why us? Who have you pissed off lately?"

"I don't care much for it myself, Dave, but there's not a lot we can do about it."

"Maybe you can't, but I'm not about to spend the rest of my career chasing a psycho that we'll never catch."

"You got a choice?"

"Yeah. I'm not going to do it."

"Don't tell me. Tell Volter."

"Fuck Volter. I'm not going to do it."

"You'll look nice in uniform."

"Fuck that. I don't give a shit. Someone else can work it."

I let him rant on for a while in the same vein until he finally ran down. "Ah, screw it," he said. "Come on over and have a drink. Christine is cooking dinner right now."

"Am I welcome with her this week?"

"You're the apple of her eye, Jase."

"Hmm. I'll bet. What are we having?"

"What do you care? It's free."

"You have a point. I'll be over in about half an hour."

On my way to Dave's house, I wondered if he had really told Christine I was coming over. She and I didn't get along too well. She didn't care much for cops as a rule anyway, which was too bad since she was married to one. It wasn't so much that she didn't like me personally as it was she felt I was a bad influence, someone just a little too uncivilized for her taste. My frequent jokes about the Mormons didn't help. She was Mormon and he wasn't, although she hadn't given up trying to convert him.

In New York City, where Dave grew up, you'd take him as a cop right away. He's got that cop habit of unconsciously glancing around every few seconds, like a driver checking his rearview mirror. Compact frame. Slicked-back dark hair. Square face and a gap between his teeth. A Brooklyn accent that twenty years in Utah hasn't touched. The frank, open countenance of a born con man. A truly infectious smile. But if you catch him off guard—not an easy thing to do—you'll see a cold and calculating hardness in his face. The quintessential Irish Catholic, stranded in a Mormon desert.

He loves to promote the image of the typical dumb cop, which he's not. It drives Christine up the wall. She can't stand him when he gets around other cops. She thinks he's better than that. When Dave and Christine finally got married, she did her best to pick more sensible friends for him to hang around with. She had managed it pretty well, and most of his friends after work were no longer cops. I couldn't really blame her. She wasn't going to be pleased to find out Dave and I were working a long-term assignment, spending a lot of time together.

Dave was on his front porch as I pulled up, talking to a young woman I didn't know. She walked down the steps as I walked up, giving me a quick, appraising glance, nodding her head gravely as she passed. Medium height, maybe five foot six, chestnut hair, a nice walk. Face a little sharp, but good bones. She was wearing a black halter top and jeans, and looked very good in them. She walked as if she knew it too. Not suggestive, just aware.

"Who's the pretty lady?" I asked, turning to watch her go.

"Her name's Jennifer. A friend of Christine's." That explained why I hadn't met her before. Christine seldom introduced me to her friends.

"She married?"

"Not that I know of."

"Boyfriend?"

"I'll tell you later. Come in and set yourself down."

Inside the house the air conditioning was on, a relief from the heat outside. I lowered myself into Dave's leather armchair, the best one in the house, and accepted a martini without too much arm twisting. Christine heard us come in and poked her head out of the kitchen.

"Hello, Jason," she said, very polite. "Nice to see you."

"Christine."

"Pot roast okay with you?"

"I guess I could manage to choke some down."

She gave me the briefest of smiles. "Dave says you two are going to be working on a special case together."

"Unless we can figure some way out of it," I said. She withdrew her head back into the kitchen. I thought I heard her mutter "good luck" under her breath, but I couldn't be sure.

Over dinner Dave finally accepted the inevitable and we hashed out a plan of action for the next few days. It was really more a plan of inaction. The only hard fact we had was the truck that had been seen when the Gilson girl was taken. So far that had been a dead end. In Salt Lake City everybody and his brother owns a pickup. We couldn't even talk to the Gilson girl witness for information. He never had given his name.

Basically, the usual homicide routine could be thrown out the window. Serial killers usually pick their victims at random, so there wasn't much point in talking to friends, relatives, boyfriends, and such. About the only place to start was with the various missing women. There was a slight chance of a link somewhere between them. Maybe they shopped at the same stores. Maybe they tended to frequent the same movie theaters, or went to the same bars, or all attended Jazz games.

Neither one of us felt very hopeful. What it came down to was that we had nothing to work with. The "investigation" would be a farce. We would just be going through the motions, waiting for the next victim. It wasn't a very cheerful prospect. I started feeling depressed, and made my excuses right after dinner. Dave walked out with me to my car, still chewing on the whole situation.

"Tell me something about that girl," I said, trying to change the subject.

"What girl?" he asked innocently.

"Oh, it's like that, is it? The girl who was here. The one on the porch. Or am I stepping on somebody's toes?"

His face lit up with sudden comprehension. "Oh, *that* girl. Jennifer."

"Jennifer," I agreed.

"Believe me, you don't want to know."

"That bad?"

"Not really. Jennifer's a real nice lady. It's just that—" He broke off suddenly and gave me a calculating look. It was the same look I had seen on his face whenever he was trying to decide how far he could push a particular scam.

"Forget it," I said hastily. "Never mind."

"Now hold on a minute, Jase. Take it easy.

Wouldn't you like to help out a lady in distress?"

"Not particularly."

"You never know. She might turn out to be extremely grateful."

"No."

"Oh, come on. At least listen to what I have to say."

"No way."

"Christine will kill me if she finds out we're even talking about this."

"You're talking. I'm leaving."

"Give me a break, will you? I'm trying to do you a favor. Jennifer is a very special lady. You would like her. You two might hit it off."

"Except that she has this problem."

"Well, yes. But it's not anything you couldn't handle. It's her boyfriend."

"Good night, Dave."

"Wait a minute, damn it, just listen. It's like this. She's been living with this guy she met about a year ago. Works for an ad agency or something. Money, a cabin up at Brighton, the whole bit. He seemed nice enough. She brought him over here once. Then he started acting real peculiar. Paranoid, like. Started accusing her of sleeping around, then claimed she was ripping him off. Finally he blamed her for his getting fired from his job."

"Speed or coke?"

"Probably both. Or maybe just psycho. Anyway, he finally took a couple of whacks at her the other night, so she moved out. She's at the Hillside Motel now. She's afraid to stay with any of her friends because he knows them all. She called him today, and he said he was going to kill her when he found out where she was."

"Wonderful."

"She's really scared, and she doesn't scare easily. She was over here for some advice."

"How about 'leave town.' "

"She can't. She's a dancer with Ririe-Woodbury, and just got the lead in their new production. There's someone coming out from San Francisco to take a look at her. If they like what they see, she gets to join their company. That's like making it to the big leagues. They don't take rain checks. If she quits now, that's it."

"And what sage and considered advice did you give her?"

"Well, all she needs is a place to stay for a couple of weeks, until this whole thing blows over, with someone around who could handle things in case there's trouble."

"Someone like me, for instance."

"It's an idea."

"Not a very good idea. What's wrong with her staying right here? I mean, she's Christine's friend, isn't she?"

Dave hesitated, looking a little embarrassed. "Actually, she did stay with us for about a week when she first got to Salt Lake."

"And?"

"And Christine overheard something I said to her, and misunderstood what it was. It made for a little coolness for a while. I don't think Jennifer's moving in here would be such a great idea."

"I see."

"There wasn't anything to 'see.' "

"Whatever you say, Dave." I shook my head. "What makes you think she would go for the idea anyway? She's never even met me."

"I'll talk to her. I'll tell her you're okay. Listen, if she wants, will you put her up for a couple of weeks, just until things calm down? Jason, she's had a lot of trouble lately, and she's worth helping. I wouldn't ask you if she wasn't, you know that."

Dave had that very earnest expression on his face he gets only when he wants something from someone. I knew I was being had, but I could still appreciate a good con job. I doubted she would take him up on the offer anyway. "Okay," I said. "On one condition."

"What's that?"

"You tell her it's your idea, not mine."

"Absolutely."

"What's Christine going to think about it?"

"Oh, she'll approve," he said airily. I realized she probably would. Better to have the girl at my house than at hers. Dave definitely had an eye for the ladies, and friendship goes only so far. "Thanks, Jase, I appreciate it," he said.

"Forget it. But you know what they say, Dave. No good deed ever goes unpunished."

TWO

For the next few days we were pretty busy, trying to get a handle on anything our supposed victims might have had in common. Dave didn't mention anything more about Jennifer, so I didn't either. I guessed it had all been straightened out. But Tuesday night about ten the phone rang.

"Hello?" I answered.

"Hello, is this Jason?" The voice was young, female, low-pitched, and rather strained.

"That's me."

"My name is Jennifer Lassen. A friend of Dave and Christine's?"

"Oh, right," I said. "Dave told me something about your situation. He said you were having a small problem with your boyfriend."

She laughed nervously. "That's what I

thought it was, a small problem. Except about an hour ago I got a call here at the motel I'm staying at. Brian, that's my boyfriend, or at least he was, found out where I am. He said he was coming over to cut my throat." Her voice got a little shaky. "He described in detail how he was going to do it. I don't know how he found out I was here. I called Dave's house, but there's no answer."

"Did you call the cops?"

"Yes, I did. Two officers came by. They just left. They were really nice, but they weren't very reassuring. They were younger than I am, for God's sake. They told me there wasn't anything they could do about it unless Brian actually came here. I can't stay here and wait for him to show up. He sounds really crazy this time."

I knew how that went. A patrol cop gets about ten calls like that every week. Someone's roommate or boyfriend or husband is always about to come over and kill them. There isn't a goddamned thing you can do about it. If you happen to be there when they show up, and they're stupid enough to threaten someone right in front of you, you can take them to jail overnight. otherwise it's just, "See you later, pal, you be on your way now." "You mean you can't do anything until he actually kills me?" is the unbelieving question every woman asks. The answer, unfortunately, is, "Yes, ma'am, that about sums it up." Thankfully, the threats are almost never carried through. But it happens. It happens. I couldn't just leave her there, in any case. I'd told Dave I would help.

"You can come over here and stay if you like," I suggested. "I've got a spare bedroom. My guess is that this guy is a lot more talk than anything else, but there's no point in taking chances. At least you'll be able to get some sleep here."

"Are you sure that's all right?"

"Any friend of Dave or Christine's is always welcome here," I told her. I didn't add that young, attractive women friends were a lot more welcome than, say, old alcoholic cop friends.

"Well, maybe I will then," she said, the relief evident in her voice. "Just for a night or two. I really appreciate it. I hate to be trouble like this. Up to now I've always been able to take care of myself without any problem."

"No trouble. Don't worry about it, these things happen. Have you got my address?"

"Dave gave it to me. I'm only about fifteen minutes away. My stuff is already packed, what I have. I don't have much. Most of my things are still at my apartment."

"Fine. I'll see you in a while then. Look for a gray Honda in the driveway."

Twenty minutes later a red Volkswagen pulled slowly down the street, looking at the addresses. I flipped on the porch light and opened the door, and the car pulled into my driveway. She got out of the car carrying a couple of large suitcases. I helped her into the house with them and she sank down on the couch with a sigh.

"God, it's funny how quickly things change. A month ago I was miserable because I didn't think I was going to get the chance to dance in San Francisco. Now just feeling safe for the night has become my highest ambition in life." She held out a slim hand. "Jennifer Lassen."

"Jason Coulter. Jase to my friends. Which do you want, a drink or some coffee?"

"Coffee. Oh, bless you, coffee would be just perfect."

I went into the kitchen and put some beans in the grinder, measured out the water, and started up the pot. As I fussed, I kept glancing over at her sitting on the couch, the typical male inspection. Jeans again and a dark pullover. The same sharp face, with humor lines around the mouth and the eyes. A little older than I had first thought. Warm eyes, gray eyes showing signs of strain, but still with that glint of self-deprecation, that mocking look that says, "Don't take me too seriously, because God knows, I certainly don't." No jewelry. Long hair past the shoulders, light brown, with a reddish tint. Nice mouth. A good smile. A good body, trim and hard without losing any femininity. From what I could see, a very good body. I brought coffee back into the living room and set a cup down in front of her. She was watching me, noticing my covert inspection.

"Well?" she said, taking a sip. "Do I pass?"

I laughed, slightly disconcerted. "Sorry. I hadn't realized I was being so obvious."

"That's okay. Cops are supposed to look carefully at people, aren't they?"

"Yes, but that wasn't exactly the way I was looking at you."

She curled her feet up under her on the couch and studied me without saying anything, returning the favor. Fair enough, I thought. I tried to look at myself through her eyes, the way I had been looking at her. Just over six feet. Almost thin, 175 at last check. Dark hair, thick, long for a cop, fairly short for anyone else. A face that the mirror told me was open, friendly, and inspiring of trust, but that friends tend to describe as guarded, wary, and bleak. Dark eyes. Watchful eyes, cautious eyes, eyes that come from looking at too many dead bodies, eyes that have watched too many people tell too many desperate lies. Not a bad face, not mean, but a little harsh, maybe. After a minute I echoed, "Well? Do I pass?"

She looked at me thoughtfully. "Dave says you're a great guy. Christine's not so sure, but she says you come through when you have to. I was trying to see it in your face."

"And do you?"

She hesitated, then smiled. "To be honest, not really. I was just thinking, if I came on the scene of a crime, and you were standing there with someone else, I'd assume you did it."

"That's very comforting."

"Actually it is. If Brian finds out somehow that I'm here, the amiable approach just isn't going to fly. He thrives on terrifying likable people. Besides, even if you look a little scary, you're actually one of the good guys. At least Dave says you are."

The chair creaked as I leaned back. "Oh, I

don't know. I don't think there are any good guys, not really."

"Probably not. But at least there are some not-so-bad guys."

"You willing to settle for that?"

"Not yet. But I'm getting closer." She put her hand over her mouth to stifle a yawn. "I thought Brian was a good guy when I met him. Everything was great for about two months. We had a lot of good times. He can be charming when he wants to be, and very nice. Then he started getting weird. He'd accuse me of sneaking out of the house to see other men when he was asleep. If he couldn't find something in the house, he'd say I took it, then he'd apologize and tell me he was sorry, he knew he was acting crazy, but he was better now. He would be extra nice and thoughtful for a couple of days. Then it would start up all over again. That was bad enough, but then he started in with . . ."

"With what?"

She laughed, embarrassed. "Oh, weird sex stuff. I'm pretty open-minded, but this was weird, believe me. Anyway, I kept telling myself the real Brian wasn't like that. It wasn't until it had gone on for quite a while that I realized his good times were the aberration, not the bad ones."

"You seem to be smarter than to get fooled like that."

"Being smart has nothing to do with it. You must know that."

"Yeah, I guess I do at that," I admitted.

Stony came bounding in through the open window. He hit the floor with a thump and broke up the conversation. Jennifer gave a start. "Sorry," she apologized. "I guess I'm still a little spooked."

Stony saw her on the couch and stopped dead. "Meet Stony," I said. "He's a little wary of new people."

"I'm not surprised. Pets tend to take on characteristics from their owners, you know."

"Yeah, but he's not a pet. He just lives here."

Of course, the minute I said Stony was cautious of new people, he walked up to her and stood up on his hind legs, putting his front paws on her knee. I expected the usual "kitty, kitty" routine, but instead she made a strangled sound in the back of her throat, a perfect mimic of an inquiring cat. Stony flattened his ears and looked up at her. She did it again and he looked over at me, put his paws back on the floor, hopped up into his favorite chair, and started cleaning himself.

"He's not impressed," I said.

"Sure he is. He'd just rather die than admit it. He's a cat."

"Yeah, but don't tell him that."

She laughed. "You know, it's nice to see a cat here, I wouldn't have expected to. Somehow, I never think of cops and cats as going together."

"Cops and Dobermans, maybe?"

She laughed again. "Something like that, I guess. Brian hates cats. That should have told me something right away." She looked at Stony cleaning himself in the chair. "I don't think I've ever seen a cat with quite those markings," she said. "He looks sort of . . . like he was assembled from used parts of other cats."

I looked at him critically. "He does, doesn't he? But speak softly. He thinks he's quite handsome—I know, don't say it. Pets tend to take after their owners."

"Maybe it's the other way around," she said. "Anyway, I think he's a fine cat." She gave another yawn. I suddenly remembered my duties as a host and showed her the spare room. Kind of bare, but adequate. Clean sheets, clean towels, an old dresser and an empty closet for clothes.

"Paradise," she sighed. "I'm going to take a quick shower and hit the sack. I'm just wiped out, and I've got early rehearsal tomorrow."

"Has your boyfriend been showing up there, too?"

"Ex-boyfriend, please. He's been there twice so far, but he hasn't done anything except stare and make me nervous." She shrugged. "Oh, well."

Jennifer yawned again, picked up her stuff and put it in the spare room. Then she went into the bathroom and I could hear water running. It was an extraordinarily pleasant sound. It had been a long while since there had been a girl in the shower. I moved over to the couch, put my feet up, and lit a cigarette. I reminded myself that she had come here for a place to hide, not for a date. I reminded myself that I didn't have the time to get involved with anyone, much less a girl with a crazy ex-boyfriend. I told myself that starting up with someone new was probably the last thing on her mind anyway.

The other side of the coin was simple. As far as the ex-boyfriend was concerned, I was already involved the minute she stepped into my house. But I wasn't thinking about him. What I was thinking about was chemistry. It's a sad commentary on the human spirit, but most of what goes on between men and women is nothing more than that. Glands and electrical impulses. Sound waves and pheromones. How someone moves. Their tone of voice, the exact pitch of their words. If it's there, it's there, and if it's not, nothing in the world can create it. Finding the right chemistry is a lot rarer than finding a good woman, and a good woman doesn't come along every day.

With Jennifer, the chemistry was there. I didn't know her. I had only talked with her for half an hour, but sometimes all you need is five minutes. All the other stuff—the stuff that ultimately makes being with a person worthwhile or not—that was still an unknown. I'd never known a woman where the chemistry and the relationship both worked. I was beginning to think the two things were mutually exclusive, at least for me. I was also beginning to suspect that it might be something in me that made things be that way, something I didn't care to look at too closely. But maybe, just maybe, I finally got some luck. She felt real, she felt solid. It was an awful lot to put on a woman I had talked to for all of half an hour. Maybe I was just creating a fantasy out of whole cloth. But I didn't think so. Not this time.

I once knew a lady who was all I ever wanted in a woman. She was bright, she was funny; a marvelous person and a total lady. And she was exceptionally good-looking. But alas—no chemistry. I loved her like the proverbial sister.

So I left her and chased instead after a vain and selfish girl who possessed nothing of worth. I didn't even like her all that much, but I kept after her all the same. I finally did stop seeing her, because my ego wouldn't let me continue, but I still caught my hand straying to the phone every now and then.

It's not just men. Women aren't any different. "Why on God's earth does she stay with *him?*" is a common wonder. Chemistry. It's not just sex, although that's a very big part of it. It's that peculiar connection that you sometimes get. It's someone you can be whole with, no matter what their flaws, if only for five minutes. If it isn't there, something's lacking. If it's there, nothing else seems to matter very much.

Jennifer came out of the bathroom wrapped in a towel and stuck her head in the living room for a moment to say good night. "Thanks again," she said. "I'll see you tomorrow, I guess."

I got up and checked outside, to make sure her boyfriend hadn't followed her from the motel. The street was quiet, and a light rain was just starting. This one might be worth some trouble, I thought. This one might be worth a whole lot of trouble. But take it easy, Jason. Don't blow it. Use some finesse for a change. Take it slow.

THREE

Next morning I woke up to the smell of coffee drifting into my room and the sound of small clankings and stirrings in the kitchen. I sat up in bed, lit a cigarette, and mused on these quiet sounds of domestic tranquillity. I thought of waiting until Jennifer left before getting up. I'm not at my best in the morning, and I didn't want to dispel any possible good impression I might have made the night before. The desire for a cup of coffee struggled with the desire to keep my image intact, until I decided I was being silly and swung my feet out onto the floor. I slipped on an old pair of Levi's and a T-shirt, staggered into the bathroom for a minute, and strolled into the kitchen, still yawning. Jennifer was sitting at the kitchen table with a cup of coffee, looking only half awake herself. I poured myself a cup and sat down at the table across from her. We stared at each other without saying a word. Finally she broke the silence.

"Thank God," she said. "I was afraid you were going to be one of those horrible cheery morning people, and I was going to have to be witty and bright."

"Do I look that bad?"

"You see how I look? You look worse. I doubt that your vocabulary even includes the words 'good morning.'"

I immediately proved her wrong. "The only good morning is a dead morning."

"Well said." She gulped the rest of her coffee and pushed back her chair. "I'm already late—the usual choice of sleep or breakfast. I can't face breakfast anyway most of the time, but it is hard to dance on an empty stomach."

I followed her into the living room. "Wait a second," I said, pulling open the desk drawer and handing her a set of keys. "The old one is for the bottom lock, the shiny new one is the top deadbolt. If I'm not here when you get back, make yourself at home. I should be back by about five-thirty."

"Okay. How about letting me cook dinner for us? I'd feel better if I thought I was earning my keep."

"Can you cook?"

"It's the thing I do second best." I raised my eyebrows, and she made a face at me. "No, I don't mean *that*. The thing I do best is dance."

"Oh."

She shook her head in amazement. "Men.

How can you think like that at this hour of the morning?"

"I didn't say a word."

"You didn't have to."

"I didn't even think it."

"Interesting," she said thoughtfully. "A pervert *and* a liar."

"Men are disgusting," I agreed.

"Yes, and that's one of their better points." We looked at each other deadpan, and then we both laughed at the same time.

"Dinner at six, then," she said.

Dave was already in the office when I showed up, sitting at the computer terminal running names.

"Make-work," he said with disgust. "Volter's idea. Friends of the various victims. 'See what you can come up with on these names,' he says. Jesus."

"What else have we got to do?"

"I know. Don't remind me."

I started leafing through the case reports that were on Dave's desk, reports on missing women from the last few months. "That girl Jennifer came over last night," I said casually. "She's going to be staying at my place for a while."

Dave stopped running names and looked up at me. "She okay?"

"So far."

"What do you think of her?"

"Seems nice enough."

He looked at me and snapped his fingers. "Son of a bitch! I knew there was something different about you this morning."

"What?"

"You were smiling when you came in. You sly dog, you."

"It's nothing like that, Dave. She's just staying there. Nothing's going on." That wasn't a lie, but it wasn't exactly the truth either.

"Sure. Just remember, if it works out, you owe me."

"And if her boyfriend comes over with a shotgun, you owe me."

"It'll never happen."

"Aren't you the same guy who told me the Jazz would never trade Dantley?"

"They didn't. They gave him away for two white guys who can't play."

"What did you expect? This is Utah."

"Don't remind me," he said for the second time, and turned back to the computer.

I picked up the reports again and started studying them. There wasn't anything in them that was any help. They all said the same thing. Woman missing, no suspects, no witnesses. Absolutely no indication of where any of them might be. Probably lying somewhere out in the west desert. A complete dead end, every one.

Nothing much got accomplished that morning, so we went out in the afternoon and interviewed the boyfriend of Sandra Gilson, the girl who disappeared from the Kelly Green Lounge. The boyfriend was cooperative, eager to help, but we didn't get anywhere. We were just tramping over old ground. No, the two of them hadn't been having any trouble. She didn't have any enemies that he knew of. He didn't own a pickup. He didn't think she knew anyone who owned a pickup. He didn't know any really fat people, except for his cousin Willie in San Diego.

"I don't know how long I can keep doing this," Dave said after we left.

"It's not as bad as sitting at a computer terminal."

"No, and it's not as bad as shoveling shit, either, but it's not going to get us anywhere."

"Cheer up," I said encouragingly. "Another girl will disappear before too much longer."

"Yeah. With no witnesses and no clues."

"Don't be so negative. Sooner or later something will turn up. Somebody will see something; somebody will talk too much. You know how it goes."

"I guess." He brightened up a little. "Maybe we'll find another body." He gave himself a little shake, like a man with a sudden chill. "Jesus, listen to me. This job really makes you into a ghoul."

"That it does."

"It fucking warps you, that's what it does."

"Shit, you were warped in the first place."

"I was not."

"Sure you were."

"No, I wasn't. God, what a job. Why do we do it, Jase?" Dave asked me that same question about twice a week, on average. I never did have any answer.

When I got home that afternoon, Jennifer was standing in front of the kitchen stove, and Stony was sitting nearby on the floor looking up at her hopefully. Whatever she was cooking, it smelled good.

"Honey, I'm home," I announced as I walked through the door. She picked it up immediately.

"That's nice, dear. Tough day at the office?"

"So-so. Not too bad. What's for dinner?"

"A surprise. Your favorite. Why don't you sit down and I'll fetch your pipe and slippers."

"I don't have a pipe and I never wear slippers."

"Then you must belong somewhere else. Try next door."

"I already did. They suggested I come over here." I bent over the pot. "Smells good. What is it?"

"Chicken and mushrooms and vegetables and stuff."

I sniffed. "Tarragon?"

"And sage and thyme."

"Maybe you can cook." I opened a cupboard. "What do you think, wine with dinner?"

"Sounds marvelous."

"White?"

"Whatever's here."

I got a bottle of Rosemont Estate Special Reserve from the cupboard, an Australian Chardonnay that had wiped out most of the French big names in a blind tasting last year, and put it on ice. Jennifer looked at the label and made approving sounds. She put the lid back on the pot. "It's still got to simmer for another hour or so."

I changed clothes, and when I came back out she was curled on the couch in the living room, one leg tucked under her, staring out the window. "Brian showed up at the studio this morning," she said.

"Any trouble?"

"No, not really. He kept smirking at me with that creepy sick smile of his until Jim Cook, our director, told him to leave or he would call the police, so Brian did. But he said that he'd just have to see me later on. It made my skin crawl. I can't believe I ever even liked him, much less . . ."

"People change."

"Not that much, they don't. I must have been totally oblivious. He made me so nervous that I drove around in circles before I came back here, trying to see if he was following me."

I looked at her thoughtfully. "Maybe it would be for the best if he did," I said. "Then I could have a little talk with him."

"God, no. You don't know what he's like."

"Oh, I don't know. I think I've got a pretty good idea. I don't think he's crazy at all. Oh, he's sick enough, all right, but not totally gone, not off the deep end crazy. He's just trying to scare you to death."

"Well, he's doing a very good job of it," she said, using an old vaudeville line. I wasn't sure if she knew it or not.

"Sure," I answered, "but look at how he's going about it. He calls you at the motel, but he doesn't come over. He knew you would call the cops. He comes over to the studio, but doesn't do anything because there are people around. He leaves when the director threatens to call the cops there. He's acting like he's crazy, but he's not out of control. He knows exactly what he's doing: making your life miserable."

"You've got that much right. I don't know, maybe you're right, but you haven't seen him. Or heard that laugh of his." She shuddered. "You don't know him."

"Maybe not, but I've seen an awful lot of people like him."

"I wonder. I still think he's crazy. If he ever did come over here, it would get ugly."

"You want to spend the rest of your life hiding from him?"

"Not really."

"You know, there aren't a whole lot of advantages to being a cop, but one of them is that you get used to dealing with unpleasant people. I don't particularly enjoy it, but it doesn't particularly bother me either."

"Are you sure you want to get that involved."

I looked at her for about five seconds and then said levelly, "I'm sure."

She got a little flustered for a moment and jumped up to run into the kitchen. "A few more minutes," she called back. "Should I open the wine?"

"Stand back," I answered. "This is man's work. Women cook and clean. Men open wine."

"Oh. Forgive me. For just the briefest of moments I forgot myself."

"No harm done," I said magnanimously. When I tried to open the bottle, the cork broke off halfway, and I ended up having to push it into the bottle. Jennifer started whistling innocently, watching with an air of total fascination. "So *that's* how it's done," she said. "You know, I always wondered."

I muttered something about sabotage and poured a couple of glasses while she dished out the chicken. It was superb. She really could cook.

We avoided the subject of Brian completely and talked about other things. Much to my delight, Jennifer turned out to be an avid basketball fan. At one time basketball was my life. I was quite the star when I was younger, fast and tricky, a good ball handler, a great passer. And although I'm just a shade over six feet, and white at that, I can still dunk the ball. It's childish, but that simple fact has given me more satisfaction than almost anything else I've accomplished in life. I even had dreams of a tryout with an NBA team until one day when I got into a pickup game with a guard who had failed to make the cut at Wyoming in the Continental league. The Continental league is the dumping grounds for all the hopefuls and has-beens who can't make the grade in the NBA. This third-rater scored 35 points on me, stole the ball four times, and generally wiped me off the court. At least I had the sense not to pursue the matter after that.

Jennifer and I shared a passion for the New York Knicks. I told her about the glory days of Willis Reed, Walt Frazier, and the rest of that perfect team. We agreed the Celtics were the most despicable team in professional sports. "The Boston Caucasians," she called them contemptuously. "If they just weren't so goddamn *good.*" We traded stories and laughed at each other. We talked life and laughed at ourselves. We were comfortable together, like old and very dear friends, but with a thousand things to discover. At one point, talking animatedly, she put her hand over mine and sent my heart rate up twenty beats. About halfway through the meal I realized I was hooked, but good. It didn't bother me in the least. Everything was so perfect that I was half expecting the phone when it rang.

"Jason?" said an all too familiar voice. "Mike Volter." Oh, Christ, I thought. Mike Volter. Just perfect.

"Yeah, Mike. What's up?"

"Another homicide just went down. State Street and 90th South."

"90th South? That's County turf. Where are the county boys?"

"They're out there. They're looking for three suspects. Three men." Volter paused. "Three men in a dark-colored pickup."

Three men in a pickup. Very interesting. "I'm on my way," I said. "Have you called Dave yet?"

"He's on his way there right now."

"You going to be out there?"

"Not unless you think you need me. Keep me advised, though."

"Will do," I said.

I put down the phone and grabbed my gun and radio. Jennifer gave me an inquiring look. "A homicide," I explained. "I probably won't be back till late. Sorry. Not the perfect end to a very nice evening."

"Certainly not the end I had in mind," she said quietly.

I started to make a quick comeback and

changed my mind when I realized she wasn't making a joke. I opened my mouth but couldn't think of anything to say. "That's okay," I said finally. "We've got lots of time."

She smiled lazily at me. "We just might have at that."

All the way down State Street I was humming. I felt great. I was on top of the world. It was still hot out, but a beautiful summer night, and I had the windows rolled down all the way. I couldn't keep the smile off my face. I had to carefully rearrange my features when I reached 90th South, though. It doesn't do to be joking and chortling around a homicide scene. For some reason it tends to upset people. They're liable to think you're strange.

I saw Dave's car pulled off to the side of the road, a little way beyond a blue Toyota that obviously had belonged to the victim. The Toyota was surrounded by marked sheriff's cars. The usual crowd of curious onlookers was being deftly herded away by the uniformed deputies, and one of them moved up to intercept me as I got out of my car. I explained who I was and showed my badge, and he moved reluctantly aside. There isn't a whole lot of love lost between city and county law enforcement, even though we actually work out of the same building, but no uniformed cop really wants to risk telling a homicide detective to butt out, no matter what the jurisdiction is. There's always the chance it might come back on him someday.

There were five or six plainclothesmen from the sheriff's office there already, taking pictures, doing measurements, interviewing people—your typical homicide investigation. The door on the driver's side of the Toyota was standing open, and next to the car was a chalk outline of a figure. In the middle of the outline was a huddled shape lying on the pavement. There was blood trailing out from under the shape, a lot of it. I suddenly didn't feel quite so cheerful anymore.

Dave was already talking to Hal Webster, one of the county homicide dicks, and he waved me over when he saw me. I didn't know Hal very well, but I did notice he was wearing the same rumpled gray suit that he'd had on the last time I had seen him, six months ago. Sweat was gleaming off his bald head. He stuck out his hand as I walked up. "Jay, isn't it? I understand you guys think there's a connection here to one of your cases."

Dave gave me a warning look, which I didn't need. I wasn't about to bring up the serial killer possibility, not yet. "Sandra Gilson," I said. "About a month ago. Three guys in a pickup is all we've got. She's missing. We're not even sure she's dead."

"Well, this girl is dead, you can bet the farm on that. And there were three guys in a pickup."

"What happened?"

"I was just telling Dave here, what we got is a witness who saw the whole thing. The guy works over at the Pay-Less across the street. He noticed the victim's car, that Toyota, when it pulled over to the side of the road. It looked to him like it had a flat tire or something." Webster gestured toward the car. I could see that it did. "He noticed it, he says, because the girl who got out of the car was a blonde, a real looker.

"He was wondering whether to go over and see if he could help—you can bet he wouldn't have bothered if she was a dog—and while he was trying to make up his mind, a pickup pulls in behind her, newer model, dark blue or green, he thinks. A couple of guys get out, so he figures his chance is gone and goes back to sorting stock or whatever the hell he was doing. About five minutes later, though, he hears a commotion outside, and when he looks out he sees three men trying to pull this girl into the truck. She's not having any part of it; she's kicking and fighting and screaming and generally carrying on. one of the men has her by the arms and the other two are trying to lift her into the truck. The guy from the store goes outside to see if he can help. They are obviously too much for him, he admits, but at least he was going to give it a try, maybe yell at them or something, for whatever good that would have done.

"Just as he steps outside the store, though, one of the men pulls out a gun. Our guy just freezes. Shit, you can't hardly blame him. The man with the gun says something to the girl, and points the gun right at her. Our guy can't hear what he says, but he can hear the reply right across the street. The girl yells, 'fuck you' at the top of her voice."

"Wrong thing to say," I remarked sadly.

"No shit. Anyway, they keep struggling with the girl, the gun goes off, and there she is, lying on the ground. The guy doesn't know if it was on purpose or an accident or what. They were all kind of bunched up together, and he couldn't see what was going on too well. The guy with the gun yells something to the other two, and they jump in the pickup and take off."

"Did he get a license?"

"Partial. An old-style plate. Last three digits."

"Can he I.D. any of them?"

"He's not sure."

"Of course not."

"He does think he might be able to I.D. one of them. Not the guy with the gun, one of the others. A big guy, he says, just enormous, with a full beard. Kind of sloppy fat."

Big and fat. Just like with Sandra Gilson. Dave looked over at me. "Sound familiar?" he said.

I walked over to the body and stared down at her. She was lying curled up on her side, head turned up, blond hair spilling out on the asphalt, covering part of her face. It looked like she had been shot in the back, just below the left shoulder blade. A small fist was still clenched defiantly. One of her shoes had come off, and blood that had oozed down from her pooled around it. There was a puzzled expression on her face. This kind of thing can't happen to me, it said. This is what happens to women on the evening news, not to people like me. I imagined her alive, joking and laughing, all warm eyes and smiling lips. I thought of Jennifer, looking at me over a glass of wine. The girl's eyes were now cold and glazed, staring up at the night sky.

I looked over as one of the uniformed deputies came to stand beside me. "What a shame," he said, looking down. "Such a pretty girl, too."

I looked back at the body and decided there was no expression on her face after all, not really. She didn't look puzzled, or angry, or frightened, or at peace. She just looked dead. I remembered the young Mexican woman lying on the table of the hospital morgue. What a waste, I thought. What a fucking waste. Ten years looking at this stuff, and I still don't understand it.

FOUR

I didn't get home until almost three A.M. Jennifer was asleep. When I woke up late the next morning she was gone, but she had left a note next to the coffee machine. "Gone to rehrsl. Bk. this aft. J."

I showed up at the office as soon as I was reasonably awake, and filled in Mike Volter on the woman who had been killed the night before. Dave was already up on the tenth floor with Hal Webster trying to get additional information. He came in as I was finishing up with Mike.

"Anything new?" I asked.

Dave shook his head. "The partial license number from that witness is still the only real lead. We're just going to have to run all the combinations. I talked to Webster, and they're going to run half of them, and we'll run the other half."

"How did you get him to agree to that?" I asked. "It makes too much sense." County people weren't noted for their cooperation with other agencies.

"Personal charm, my man, personal charm."

The license plate was a good break, better than we could have reasonably hoped for. Older truck licenses in Utah consist of two letters and four digits, such as PA 4402. The witness at the Pay-Less could remember only the last three numbers, but he was positive about them: 762. Running through the computer every possible variation of plates that included those last three numbers would take quite some time, though. There were, to be exact, 6,760 possible combinations.

It wasn't as bad as I thought it was going to be, since we had split up the work. A lot of the combinations were voids—no record found—plate numbers not assigned to anyone. Some of the others were older models, or little Japanese jobs. That cut down the field even further. Still others were registered downstate. That didn't totally eliminate them, of course, but they were something to be put on the back burner until the more obvious choices didn't pan out.

It took us about six hours. When we were through, we had about four hundred possibles, including the list from the county. Running the names of the registered owners for criminal records took another couple of hours. We finally came up with fifteen names that looked good, all of whom had been convicted at one time or another of violent crimes. The theory was that anyone capable of these kinds of murders was not going to be clean. They'd have some kind of record. People rarely start out full-blown as killers. They work up to it, and you can usually find their early footprints somewhere along the way.

A call to the prison eliminated six names, guys who were still out there serving their time. A little more checking eliminated two others, recently deceased. That left eight. Of course, none of this was certain. The truck might have been borrowed. The plates might have been switched. The killers might have no previous criminal history, although that wasn't likely. At this point it was all supposition. Dave wanted to get right on checking out the list of the names, but I convinced him it was better to get a fresh start in the morning. I wanted to get home and see Jennifer. Despite my reassurances to her about Brian and his intentions, I was actually a little worried about leaving her alone.

When I pulled up in my driveway, her car wasn't there. I was a little disappointed and even felt a small twinge of apprehension. Jennifer's note was still by the coffee maker, so she hadn't been back yet. Before I had a chance to get worried, I heard a *put-putting* and her red Volkswagen pulled up in front of the house. She jumped out and hurried up the walk, looking over her shoulder. Just as she reached the front door, a white Audi pulled up behind her car. I opened the door as she came in.

"Brian," she explained breathlessly. "He

started following me and I couldn't shake him, so I remembered what you said and took you at your word." She looked up at me anxiously. "Is it okay?"

I stood in the doorway, letting him see there was someone else in the house. He had started to get out of his car, but when he saw me he sank back in the seat and just sat there, grinning.

"It's just fine," I reassured her. "Just fine."

I went into my bedroom and got my Walther .380, a PPK/S, out of the bed table drawer. The department issues a Smith & Wesson .38 snub-nosed revolver to plainclothes cops, and they won't let you carry anything else, but this was private business. If Brian ever made a complaint, I was going to deny everything anyway. I took the clip out, ejected the round that was in the chamber, and put the clip back in. Jennifer followed me into the bedroom.

"My God," she said, horrified. "You're not going to shoot him, are you?"

I laughed. "No, not unless he shoots me first."

I stuck the Walther in my belt and walked out to Brian's car. He just sat there smiling at me through the open window. Jennifer was right. There was something creepy about that smile. In fact, there was something creepy about all of him. I didn't say anything; I just stood there studying him.

He looked pretty normal at first glance, longish dark blond hair carefully styled, mustache neatly trimmed, rather good-looking in a Robert Redford sort of way. It was hard to tell with him sitting down, but he didn't look very big, maybe five foot eight, five foot nine. That was lucky; it was going to make things a lot easier. There was definitely something wrong with him, though. After you've been a cop for a while, if you're any good, you can spot the wrong ones almost every time.

There are people who are so far out there that the minute they walk into a room, conversation stops. When they leave, people ask, "Who the hell was *that?*" It isn't anything they do, exactly, it's just something that seems to radiate out from them, setting off alarms in your body's awareness system. Everyone has this sense in some degree; cops just use it more, and get attuned to smaller disturbances in the psyche. Good doctors have it in a different way. A cancer specialist can often tell the first time a patient walks through the door. "The bad look," they call it.

Brian sat there smiling easily at me. I didn't smile back. Finally, to show his unconcern, he casually looked away, which was just what I was waiting for. I reached out, grabbed a double handful of thick hair, and using all my strength in an explosive effort, jerked him up out of the seat right through the open car window. It scraped him up a little and he started squawking. A quick twist threw him on his back onto the ground, and before he could get up, I had my gun out and was kneeling on his chest. I stuck the barrel roughly into his mouth. He twisted his head, trying to get away from it, so I grabbed him by the hair again with my free hand and went into my psycho act.

"You son of a bitch!" I screamed. "You worthless prick! Motherfucker, you're a dead man." I jammed the muzzle of the gun almost into his throat and cocked the hammer back on the empty chamber. The minute he heard that click, he stopped struggling and lay there without moving a muscle. There's something about the sound of that hammer cocking that makes your muscles go weak, that makes you want desperately to stay motionless and silent until it goes away. I know.

"Listen," I hissed, "and listen good. If you ever come over here again, I'll kill you. If I ever see you again, I'll kill you. If you so much as even talk to her again, I'll kill you, so help me God." I paused, and my hands were shaking. When you throw yourself into a role like this, you have to be careful it doesn't get out of hand. I was starting to believe it myself. "What the fuck," I said coldly. "What's the point of waiting? Screw it, I think I'll just kill you right here and now."

I moved the gun again for emphasis and he started making inarticulate mewling sounds. I had to suppress a strong desire to laugh.

"Shut up," I snarled. "Shut up, you asshole. No, I'm not going to kill you. I should, but I'm not going to. Not yet. Not this time." I pulled his head up a little and put my face inches from his. "Not this time," I repeated, almost whispering. "Next time. Count on it, Brian. Count on it."

I let go of his hair, and his head thudded back on the lawn. As I stood up over him, breathing hard, I noted with professional pride that he had wet himself thoroughly. I must have been convincing. Without another word

I walked away, back into the house, slamming the door behind me.

Brian lay there on the grass for about two minutes without moving. Finally he got unsteadily to his feet. He tottered back over to his car, walking like an old man. He got in carefully, sat there for a couple minutes more, and then drove away slowly.

Jennifer turned away from the window where she had been watching the whole thing. She waited until Brian drove out of sight before she spoke.

"Very impressive," she said. There was an edge to her voice.

"Something wrong?"

"I guess not."

"You upset?"

"No."

"Then why do I get the feeling you disapprove so strongly?"

"I don't, really. It's just . . ."

"Just what?"

"Just . . . did you have to do it like that?"

I had been feeling a little funny about it myself. I hadn't been as much in control as I'd thought. Also, I had enjoyed it. That made me a little uncomfortable.

"What the hell did you expect?" I said defensively. "Maybe I should have asked him ever so politely to stop ruining your life? Appeal to his better nature? Sit down and have a heart-to-heart talk with him?" She looked back out the window and didn't say anything. "Jesus Christ, Jennifer."

She turned back and faced me, sighing audibly. "I'm sorry, Jason. It shook me a little, that's all. I know I'm acting ridiculous." She looked at me sadly. "Only, did you have to enjoy what you were doing quite so goddamn much?"

I stared at her. The unfairness of it all left me speechless. I had just put myself way out on a limb to take care of her problem with Brian, and now I was getting shit for doing so.

It didn't help that she was right, either.

"That's not fair," I said, still angry.

"No? Think about it, Jason."

I thought about it. I thought about the adrenaline rush I got when I pulled him through the window. I remembered wanting to laugh when he started sputtering. I thought about the satisfaction I felt when I walked away, the conquering hero.

"I guess maybe I did enjoy it, a little," I admitted slowly.

She looked at me for what seemed like a long, long time. I looked back at her and finally shrugged. "You remember what I said the other day? There really aren't any good guys."

She spread her hands in a gesture of resignation. "Oh, well. It was just the look on your face. It scared me. It was like—well, I had this whole image of what you were like, and it suddenly dissolved in front of my eyes. When you pulled Brian through the window—" Her voice broke, and she started chewing her lip. She twisted up her face, trying not to cry. I sat there and watched, confused and hurt, until I suddenly realized what was happening. She wasn't trying not to cry. She was trying very hard not to laugh.

"When you pulled Br-Brian . . ." She finally gave up and started giggling helplessly. "Di-did you see the look on his face when he came through that window?" she said between breaths. "He looked like a goldfish yanked out of its pond. He—oh, my God, I'm as bad as you are. It wasn't funny. It was awful. Poor Brian—" She dissolved into laughter again, and I joined her. We both sat there roaring, holding on to each other, until she finally got control of herself.

"I don't know what's wrong with me," she said, wiping her eyes. "I'm ashamed of myself. It really wasn't funny. It was horrible." She started giggling again.

"The two aren't mutually exclusive," I reminded her.

"God, sometimes I'm such a prig. I'm really sorry. Forgive me, Jason."

"Forget it."

"Mind you, I still think you didn't need to get such a kick out of it."

"You're probably right. Next time I'll try to be more grim."

"Good. Then I can complain again. I'll ask why you can't lighten up once in a while."

We decided to celebrate Jennifer's release from bondage and went out to dinner at La Cloche, one of Salt Lake's few French restaurants. The food was almost as good as it would have been in San Francisco or New York, you didn't have to dress, and it cost only a third as much. There are some advantages to living in the Mountain West. There was still a slight air of awkwardness between us, left over from the afternoon. That comfortable feeling of intimacy wasn't quite there. She acted like she was expecting me to explode again at any minute. But after a while it eased and we started talking.

I told Jennifer about the case Dave and I were working on, and how it looked as though we might have a break. She was both fascinated and disturbed. I started telling her about the girl and the truck. She asked me to stop. She didn't want to hear the details. Then she decided she did. She listened carefully.

"If the girl hadn't fought, she'd still be alive, then," she said, reflecting.

"No, I don't think that's true. I think she did the best she could. If someone's trying to force you into a car, you can't just let them do it. Fight. Struggle. Scream. Go limp, whatever. But don't get into the car."

"But they had a gun," she protested. "And they killed her when she started struggling."

"True. But most of the time, the guy isn't going to be crazy enough to shoot you right there on the street. If he's enough of a psycho to do that, like these guys were, he's going to take you up one of the canyons and kill you there anyway, probably after some extremely unpleasant business. So whatever you do, even if they have a gun, *especially* if they have a gun, don't just meekly get into the car."

She was silent for a moment, looking thoughtful. "What made you become a cop, anyway?" she suddenly asked.

"I don't know. I just sort of fell into it."

"Do you like it?"

"Sometimes. Most of the time. I'm good at it."

"It doesn't fit somehow."

"What? Me being a cop?"

"Yeah."

"Why? What are cops like?"

"I don't know, really. Not like you."

"Are you sure? What about Brian this afternoon?"

"That was different. You were just acting." She leaned across the table and grabbed my arm. "You were, weren't you?"

"Mostly. Not entirely."

She relaxed and leaned back again. "You scared the shit out of me, you know. That's why I got on you."

"That was the general idea. Not you, Brian. Someone has to call people like that. Otherwise they just keep pulling their weird trip. Then one day they go a little overboard and someone gets hurt."

"I guess so." She toyed with her fork. "Is that why you do it?"

"Do what?"

"You know, stuff like with Brian. The whole cop thing."

"Partly. Maybe it's just a power trip. An authoritarian personality compensating for a weak self-esteem. Didn't you ever take any sociology classes?"

"Come on, Jase, be serious."

"I'm not sure I remember how."

"I'm not sure you want to remember how."

"Let's just say it's important for someone to deal with the human sharks in this world. Most people can't. If you can, it's sort of an obligation that you do so."

Jennifer looked at me for a long time. "I understand, in a way. But it seems like an awfully negative way to live."

"That it is," I said. "That it is."

We turned the conversation to more comfortable things and finished dinner on a more pleasant note. I had to get an early start in the morning, so we went right home after dinner. I poured us a couple of brandies for a nightcap and turned on the ten o'clock news. There was an interview with Hal Webster about the murdered girl, and he gave them the same old stuff about following up on some leads. Jennifer watched intently, fascinated.

"It's different when you know something about it, isn't it?" she said. "It's not like a news report. It makes it real, like it was someone I knew."

"Ah, you feel it too. That's one of the reasons people become cops, you know. It's not the power trip. It's the being in on stuff, knowing the real story. It can be very seductive."

"I can see that. It could really pull you in."

"Kind of like being a drug addict."

"You said it, not me. I can see it, though."

When the news was over, I yawned and stretched elaborately. "I'd really better get to bed," I said. "I've got an early day tomorrow. We've got a lot of things to do, and Dave's already champing at the bit."

Jennifer sat there swinging one leg back and forth. "Sounds reasonable," she said, pushing her hair back out of her face. "it's late rehearsal tomorrow and I can sleep in, so I guess

I'll stay up for a while. There must be something on the late movie."

"Reruns of 'Kojak,' I think."

"Oh. Well, there's always Letterman."

"Yeah. Okay. Well, I guess it's good night then."

"Good night, Jason." She let me get as far as the bedroom door before she called out.

"Jason. Wait a minute. Didn't you forget something?"

"Did I?" I waited in the doorway.

"How about kissing me good night?"

I walked back to her, bent down and kissed her gently on the lips. I moved back about half an inch, and when she didn't move, kissed her again, a little more seriously this time, and she put her hand lightly on the back of my neck. After a minute I straightened up. "What do you think about continuing this somewhere else?" I suggested, a little hoarsely.

She nodded and took me by the hand. We headed toward the bedroom, stopping once along the way to kiss again. Once there, Jennifer sat down on the bed, crossed her hands, and pulled the T-shirt she was wearing over her head. Then she eased out of her jeans and lay back on the bed, totally unselfconscious. There wasn't anything under the shirt or jeans but skin. In the glow of light coming through the open doorway, her face was almost hidden. She lay partly on one side, the shadowy soft triangle between her legs barely visible, slightly darker than her head. Stomach flat. Legs strong and smooth. Breasts not large, but high and taut. Dark areas around the nipples.

Smooth skin. A dancer's body, relaxed and comfortable.

"Well," she said, smiling from the shadows, "do I pass?"

"My God. I'd like to see you in a leotard."

"Hmm. Definite deviant leanings."

"Just give me half a chance."

She drew back the sheet and slipped under it. I got rid of my clothes and joined her there. She rolled over toward me, gently pulling me close to her. We lay there face to face, the length of her body pressed along the length of mine, warm, soft, yielding, those incredible dancer's muscles evident right beneath the surface of her skin. My hands moved slowly up and down her back. It felt better than I could have ever imagined. For a long time we were almost motionless. Then a kiss, slow at first, soon with more urgency and passion.

Most of the time the first time isn't all that great. Neither person really knows the other, or which movements and pressures are right and which are wrong, which touchings and strokings are exciting, which merely distracting. The best you can reasonably hope for is that it goes fairly well. But sometimes, once in a very great while, the first time is a total delight. Everything is right. The wonderful excitement of a new lover; the understanding of an old lover in an unspoken awareness. She was quiet and intense, not needing the usual little gasps and mutterings to tell me what was working for her. I could feel it through her body, the very tone of muscle and sinew. At the final moment she arched, let out a great sigh, and put her hand on the small of my back, drawing me still closer. We lay there for a while, quiet and spent. Finally I sat up and reached for a cigarette. Neither of us spoke. She sat up beside me and reached out for it.

"You don't smoke," I reminded her.

"I used to. I can't and still dance, but every once in a while I take a puff. On special occasions."

I handed it over to her and she took a long drag, choking a little, but obviously relishing the chance. I felt I ought to say something, but I didn't know what. Anything you say after making love sounds either like a line or sappy and sentimental. "That was very nice," doesn't seem to cover it adequately. "That was the best fuck I ever had," somehow doesn't strike the right tone either. And saying nothing can be all too easily misinterpreted. Jennifer gave back the cigarette, stretched out her hand and began drawing little circles on my knee with her finger. We lay there in silence, passing the cigarette back and forth.

"That wasn't the way I thought it would be," she said.

"Disappointed?"

"You know better. Don't fish for compliments. It was ... different than I thought it would be, that's all." She pulled the sheet up over her head and mumbled something. I pulled it back down.

"You said something."

She looked embarrassed. "I said, 'and better.' " She pulled the sheet back over her face. I put out the cigarette and ran my hand along her back. She made a little sound of encouragement and pulled the sheet down again.

"To tell the truth," I said, "I'm kind of stunned, myself. It was something, wasn't it?"

Jennifer smiled. "Almost enough to make a person believe in love." She looked at me quickly. "Don't let me scare you, Jason."

"But it does scare me. Suppose we got married and did this every night? I wouldn't survive a year."

"Married people don't do it every night."

"Then I don't ever want to get married."

"Shut up," she said, and I reached for her again.

FIVE

Neither one of us got much sleep that night, but I still had to get up in the morning. I slipped out of bed at seven, having had about two hours' sleep, and looked enviously at Jennifer slumbering away, blissfully unaware. I didn't even have time for coffee, so I stopped at a 7-Eleven and took a cup with me. At the station I picked up Dave, and we got started checking our list of names. He gave me a knowing look.

"You look a little tired this morning, partner."

"Yeah, I am."

"You been busy or something?"

"No, I just had a little trouble getting to sleep last night."

"Oh? Problems?"

"No, nothing like that. Just didn't get much sleep." I wasn't trying to be coy, I just didn't want to share anything with anyone right now, not even Dave. I wanted to savor it alone for a while.

We started driving around the valley checking on pickups from the addresses off the computer. Some of the trucks were easy to spot and eliminate. One of them, which belonged to a guy with two rape convictions, was bright red and had enough rust on the body to be sure it hadn't been recently painted. Another was dressed out with superwide mags, jacked up high off the ground, impossible to mistake for an ordinary pickup. We called the county dicks and found they had eliminated a few more.

By the end of the day we were down to three names. The one that interested me most was a guy named Jack Holzer. We had his rap sheet: twenty-seven years old, an arrest in 1982 for attempted murder, which he pled down to aggravated assault, and a couple of minor dope busts. Also one arrest in California for sexual abuse, still pending. That could mean anything from attempted rape to pinching a lady on a bus. The rap sheet had him listed as five foot ten, one sixty-five, so he couldn't be the fat guy, but he could be one of the others. His mug shot looked pretty tame, considering.

There wasn't any truck to be seen at his house, but there were a couple of choppers in the driveway, big Harleys. His neighbors on both sides knew him and didn't like him much. One of them didn't want to talk to us, but the other, a retired railroad worker with crooked teeth and one bad leg, was a lot more helpful.

"Holzer?" he said. "Yeah, I know him. He's a biker." The man pronounced the word like, "backer," and I had a sudden maniac vision of Holzer putting up the money for a Broadway show. The man spit on the ground. "What's he done?"

"We're not sure he's done anything," said Dave. "We just want to find out a little about him."

The man spit again. "Not much to tell. Haven't seen him in a few days. He's not at his house very much. He's a biker."

"Has he got a pickup truck?"

"Yeah, he does. I thought those bikers just rode motorcycles, but he's got a truck. Keeps parking it in front of my house. Asked him why didn't he park it in front of his own house, and he told me to get fucked."

"That figures," said Dave. "He's a biker, you know." The man looked at him suspiciously, not sure if he was being made fun of. I gave Dave a look and broke in quickly.

"What color is his truck?"

"Couldn't really say offhand. I think it's brown. Could be green."

"Light-colored?"

"Naw, dark. Might be blue, now that I think about it. But it's dark, that's why I can't really recall the color. You gonna arrest him?"

"Any reason we should?"

"Well, he's a biker, ain't he?"

There wasn't much else the man could tell us, but the description of the pickup helped. I was starting to get a feeling about Holzer.

Since he apparently was a "backer," I thought I'd give Brenda a call. Brenda was a C.I. of mine, a confidential informant. In other words, a snitch. If anyone knew about him, she would. Brenda really liked bikers and spent most of her time hanging out with the Pharaohs, one of the local clubs. She had been around for years, all the bikers knew her, and she heard almost everything that happened in the biker world, from idle gossip to absolute fact. I had helped her out of a sticky situation once, and she usually would fill me in when I needed to know something about the clubs. Sometimes it was a straight trade, something for something, but a lot of the time she told me things just for the hell of it. She liked the feeling of being in on things, playing the cops-and-robbers game. There are a lot of people like that.

She didn't look like what you would imagine a biker groupie would look like, either. Twenty-five, maybe, five feet two, sweet and innocent, delicate red hair and a perpetually wistful expression—that was the front she presented to the outside world. She looked absolutely straight, and in fact, held a straight job during the week working for an insurance firm. Weekends were a different story. Brenda knew every biker and sleaze in the city, and did more drugs than any human being has a right to and still be alive. She was actually a fairly nice girl, considering. She just happened to like drugs and bikers more than she did accountants and picnics.

I called her at work from the station and was told she hadn't come in that day. There was no answer when I tried her at home. I was sitting there trying to think where she might be, when Sam Woolfe from robbery caught me.

"Hey, Jason, do you know a girl named Brenda DeVore?" he asked. Talk about timing.

"Yeah. I've talked with her a few times."

"Well, she wants to talk to you now. She's down at the jail. I just finished interviewing her, but she wouldn't talk to me. Said she wanted to talk to you first."

"What have you got her on?"

"Kidnapping and aggravated robbery."

"Brenda?" I laughed in disbelief. "No way. That's not her style."

"Maybe not, but I'm screening the case tomorrow morning. Her and four teenage kids, eighteen and nineteen."

"Do me a favor, will you? Hold off until I talk to her and find out what happened?"

"She one of your snitches?"

"Just a lady who likes to do her civic duty once in a while."

"I'll bet. Nice-looking girl."

"Forget it. She's not your type."

"Yeah? Why not?"

"She's over fifteen, for one thing."

"That's a shame. Forget it then. Tell me what you find out, will you?"

I didn't know what the story was, but it had to be something flaky. Brenda didn't go in for crimes of violence. For that matter, she didn't hang around with teenagers either. Downstairs at the jail I got the matron to bring her up to the interview room. She came in looking dragged out and worn, but perked up the minute she saw me.

"Jason," she said, "am I glad to see you. This is bullshit. You've got to get me out of here. I could lose my job if they find out about this at work."

"Lose your job? I don't know, Brenda. Robbery and kidnapping charges? This could be it. This could be the big one. You might spend the rest of your life out at the Big House."

"Come on, Jason, this isn't funny."

"No, it isn't. Typical, though. A tragic case of a wasted life, I'd say."

"Jason!"

"Okay, okay. What happened?"

"You know my house? I've got the upstairs, and there's like an apartment downstairs?"

I nodded.

"About a month ago a bunch of young kids moved into the downstairs apartment. Punk rockers. You know, spike hair, earrings, the whole bit. Really weird."

"Weird, eh? Not like the average Joe Citizen you usually spend your time with."

Brenda gave me a dirty look and went on.

"Well, they're pretty nice kids really, and we got high together a couple of times. One of them, Tony, asked me if I knew where they could get some smack. None of them had ever tried any and they wanted to. I told them no, they ought to stay away from that shit anyway, but they kept bugging me about it. Finally I told them I'd see what I could do, you know, just to get them off my back. You know Felix Guevarra?"

"Little guy? Burglar?"

"Yeah, that's him. He's a junkie, too. He used to sell junk to Chico." Chico was president of the Pharaohs. He wasn't Chicano, despite his name. His legal name was Stanley Carter. Brenda once told me that Chico Marx was his favorite actor when he was a kid, that's why he took the name. I'd had a lot of dealings with Chico over the years. I even almost had a grudging respect for him.

"Felix was over one night, and I mentioned to him that the guys downstairs wanted to score some smack. He says fine, he knows a guy who's holding, and we all get into Tony's car and drive over to the west side. Tony gives Felix a hundred dollars, and Felix goes into this house alone to get the stuff."

"Brenda, Brenda," I said. "I thought you'd been around for a while."

"Fuck, it wasn't my money. I didn't even want to be there. I was just trying to do somebody a favor. Anyway, Felix never comes out. We wait about half an hour, and then Tony goes up and knocks on the door, and of course the guy there says he doesn't know anything about it and slams the door. Tony's really pissed, but what can he do? So we're driving home down North Temple, and here's Felix, walking down the street like nothing's happened. The next thing I know, Tony jumps out of the car and pulls out a fuckin' gun. I just about shit, swear to God. He starts waving it around and tells Felix they're going back to the house and get either the money or the dope.

"Felix says, 'Sure, sure, man, no problem,' and we're headed back there when this cop pulls up alongside of us. Everybody's trying to be real cool, and then Felix starts yelling, 'Help, help, I'm being kidnapped,' and shit like that. So of course the cop pulls us over, and he's pretty skeptical about the whole thing until he looks under the front seat and finds Tony's gun. The next thing I knew, we're all stretched out on the ground and about fourteen cops show up, and I'm getting searched by some dyke, and I end up in the slammer. It's not funny, Coulter!"

Brenda directed this last comment at me because I finally couldn't help laughing. "This time it's the Big House for sure, Brenda," I told her. "It's the end of the road for you."

She wasn't in any mood for jokes. "Hey, are you going to help me out or what?" she demanded.

"Relax, Brenda."

"Relax? You're not the one who's in here."

"Take it easy. I'll have you out of here by tomorrow morning. I'll get the charges dropped."

"You're kidding. You can do that? Just like that?"

Most of the time you can't do that. But as Brenda said, this was a bullshit case, and as soon as I explained what happened to Woolfe, he'd get a kick-out letter and cut her loose. Felix Guevarra wasn't going to show up to sign a complaint anyway. I was pretty sure he was still on parole. He wouldn't be too eager to explain the situation to his parole officer. But there wasn't any reason to tell all that to Brenda.

"Sure, I can do that," I said. "No problem."

I put my elbows on the table between us. "As long as I'm here, though, maybe you can help me out with something."

"Oh, right, here it comes. What do you want to know this time?"

"Hey, if you don't want to help . . ."

"Okay, Jason. I get the picture."

"Do you know a guy named Jack Holzer?"

"Holzer? You better believe I know him. He broke my jaw once. That guy is a real fucker, mean as a snake. Listen, you know all that bullshit people believe about bikers? That they spend all their time raping women and shooting smack and torturing old ladies and all that crap? Well, Holzer is really like that. He is one sick puppy."

"Who does he hang with?"

"Nobody really. I mean, he's one of the Pharaohs and everything, but nobody likes to be around him much. He's that mean. Mostly he goes around with his cousin, Fat Eddie."

"Fat Eddie?"

"Yeah. I don't know his real name. All I know is Fat Eddie. He's not even a biker, he just hangs out a lot."

"What's his trip?"

"Eddie's a real psycho. Holzer, he's not really crazy, you know? He does these crazy things, but he's always thinking. He's sick, but he's smart. Fat Eddie is just gross and stupid. He'll do anything Holzer tells him. He's a real ugly fucker too, big, super heavy. That's why they call him Fat Eddie. He's as fat as a pig, but he's strong, and he's got this big, bushy beard all over his face. He looks more like a biker than Holzer does."

"They sound like a real sweet pair."

"Yeah, they are. I heard this story where a girl pissed off Holzer about something, so he told Eddie to rape her, and Eddie did it."

"Sick," I said. "But not particularly unusual. Not for bikers."

Brenda gave me a crooked smile. "Yeah, only the girl happened to be Eddie's own sister."

"Okay, so they're a little weird," I admitted. "Who else would they be running with?"

Brenda looked at me appraisingly. "Why all this interest in Holzer and his friends?"

"Just curious."

"Uh-huh."

"Who else?" I repeated.

She thought for a minute. "I can't really think of anyone in particular. I did hear something a couple of days ago, though, something a little funny."

"About what?" I asked casually.

"Something about Holzer and his lawyer."

That threw me for a second. "What do you mean, his lawyer?" I asked.

"I mean his lawyer. Chico was talking about it down at the clubhouse. He stopped when I came in the room, but it was something about Holzer and his lawyer doing something together."

"Legal-type stuff?"

"I don't think so. It sounded like they were out somewhere, and something happened to them, or maybe they did something to someone. I wasn't really paying much attention."

"Any idea what it was?"

"I don't know, really. Chico was just saying

something like, 'Can you believe it, his own fucking lawyer was with him? They must have been crazy.' That's all I heard, honest."

"This lawyer got a name?"

"I didn't hear."

I let it ride for the moment. "Anything else you can think of? Anybody else Holzer's been with lately?"

She shook her head. "Not that I know of."

I stood up to leave and buzzed the matron that I was finished. "Thanks, Brenda," I said. "It's a help."

"You gonna tell me what this is about?"

"I don't know yet. May be nothing." The matron came into the room, took Brenda by the arm, and started leading her back to the cell tier. Brenda stopped in the doorway and turned back to me.

"Oh, one more thing," she said. "When Chico was talking about Holzer, he mentioned a girl named Julie."

"Yeah?"

"'Julie said to stay cool,' something like that. Holzer used to have an old lady named Julie. I don't know if that helps you any."

"It might. You never know."

"You won't forget about me in here, will you?"

"Not a chance, kid. You'll be out tomorrow morning."

After I left the jail, I picked up Dave and we drove around for a while and talked it over. There wasn't much doubt in our minds that Holzer and Fat Eddie were our boys. The last three license numbers matched, the truck description matched, and the witness had described a big, fat guy with a bushy beard, a good picture of Fat Eddie. Usually, things don't fit together so neatly, or come together so quickly, but it can happen that way. The business about the lawyer was kind of funny, though. It was worth taking a look at.

It would be easy enough to find out Fat Eddie's straight name and do a photo spread for the witness at the Pay-Less, but since it was officially Webster's case, we decided instead to give him that lead. In the meantime there was something else I wanted to check out.

We drove over to the courthouse and went into the records room. The clerk in charge there was a little old lady, far before her time. She couldn't have been more than thirty, but her hair was already beginning to gray and she hunched over slightly when she walked. Her mouth was twisted up in a harsh and bitter expression, and her eyes gleamed distrustfully from behind a pair of plain wire-rimmed glasses. I used to wonder how the crabby little old ladies of the world get that way. What tragedies of life could have possibly warped them so badly? What grim troubles must they have seen, what disappointments must they have felt? After pondering this for a while, I came to the conclusion that nothing much had ever happened to them at all. They were just born that way, much the same at five and at fifty. It was just the way they were. Somehow, the realization was obscurely cheering.

This particular one intercepted us as we walked through the door.

"Can I help you gentlemen?" she snapped in

a tone that made it clear she was hoping the answer would be no. Dave showed her his badge and explained we wanted to look at some of the court records. She peered at the badge suspiciously, hoping to find a reason to send us packing, but finally gave in.

"In the back," she said tersely, and motioned ungraciously toward the next room. Inside were row upon row of file folders, each containing the records of a single court proceeding, everything from multiple homicide to shoplifting. I started looking down the rows of folders on the nearest wall.

"Just what exactly are you looking for?" she asked, annoyed.

"A case from 1983—83-4065."

She shook her head, disgusted. "Well, you won't find it there. Those are all cases up to and including 1980. Cases past 1980 are against the other wall."

She clucked her tongue against the roof of her mouth, finding it hard to believe how ignorant I was, and swept out of the room. I shuddered to think of the petty fiefdom she would have established here by the time she was sixty. Maybe everything would be on computers by then. I had a feeling that she would be the only one who knew the access code, and she would not be generous in handing it out.

I found one of the cases I was looking for, the aggravated assault charge on Holzer, and pulled out the file. I had already read the police report, but there was one thing not in the report that I was very much interested in. I leafed through a few pages, and there it was, just like it was supposed to be. That never fails to amaze me. The attorney of record in the case was Julian P. Allred.

Dave had been looking on the other wall and came up with an earlier case on Holzer, a possession case, something stupid like a gram of cocaine. Holzer had once again been represented by one Julian P. Allred. We put back the files and thanked the little old lady, who immediately scurried into the back room to make sure we hadn't stolen anything, or worse, misplaced the folders.

I knew Allred slightly, having faced him in court a few times. Several years ago, when I was doing a stint in narcotics, we busted a methamphetamine lab on the west side of the city and recovered about five pounds of crank. Lying on the floor of the lab were a whole bunch of expensive tools, borrowed by the lab operator. They were engraved, and the engraving on them read, "J. Allred." Allred later represented the guy we busted when the case came to trial. He didn't get him off, but it was a close thing. He was a smart lawyer. He obviously wasn't straight, but it was hard to believe he could be involved in something this grotesque. Dave voiced the same reservations.

"What do you think?" he asked, frowning. "Is it possible?"

"Anything's possible."

"How could Allred get mixed up with someone like Jack Holzer?"

"Who knows? Maybe none of his lawyer friends are all that interested in rape and murder."

"Isn't that stretching things a bit? Just because he's represented Holzer in court a couple of times doesn't necessarily mean anything."

"True enough, but think about this. Chico was talking about Holzer and his lawyer doing something together, something crazy. That's not the kind of thing you make up out of the blue, saying a guy's lawyer was with him. We know what Holzer's been doing. What the hell do you think Allred's been doing while he's with him? Providing legal service?"

"I get the point. But it doesn't have to be Allred who was with him. It could be some other lawyer they were talking about."

"Like who?"

"Shit, I don't know. Anyone."

"Maybe, but I still think Allred's a good bet. We know he's dirty. Tell you what, why don't we give him a little push?"

"Like how?"

"Well, there's no point in confronting Allred directly. Most people, we hit them unexpectedly with something heavy and they react, right? Maybe just for a second, but they can't hide that flash. They need a moment to get their mask on straight."

"But you don't think Allred will?"

"No, I don't. Allred's a lawyer, remember. He's very used to courtroom surprises. He's practiced and able at keeping his emotions tight and his features under control. Hit him with a bomb, and no matter how shook he is inside, he'll smile blandly and ask us what the hell we're talking about. It won't tell us a thing. The only chance we've got is that right now he doesn't have the slightest idea anyone might be on to him."

"If he's really involved, that is."

"Well, yeah. That's what we're trying to find out."

"Oh. I forgot."

I ignored the sarcasm. "As soon as we start talking to Holzer or Fat Eddie, Allred will go on red alert. But right now, we might be able to throw one past him."

"Such as?"

"Watch and learn, partner, watch and learn."

It was three-thirty, so Allred ought to be out of court by now but still in his office. I stopped at a 7-Eleven, looked up his office number, and dialed. The phone was answered by a secretary with a bright, cheerful voice.

"Good afternoon, Allred and Young. May I help you?"

"Yes," I said. "Is Mr. Allred available? I would like to consult with him about representing me in court on a criminal charge."

I didn't want to talk to Allred directly. If the secretary put me right through, I would have to give him some kind of phony story and try again later. He was a pretty successful attorney, though. The chances were slim that he would be conveniently free, especially to someone he didn't know.

"I'm sorry," she said. "Mr. Allred is with a client right now. If you would like to leave your name and number, he will get back to you as soon as he can."

"That's all right. I'll try later."

I hung up the phone, waited a minute, and

dialed the number again. I got the same secretary with the same cheerful voice.

"Allred and Young. May I help you?" I noticed that she had left out the "good afternoon"
this time. Maybe she was getting ready to go
home.

"Yeah," I said, using a rougher voice. "Let
me talk to Allred."

"I'm sorry, he's with a client right now.
Could I help you with anything?"

"No. Yeah. Give him a message. Tell him
that someone who knows him saw us in the
truck Tuesday night. Have him call me immediately. This is urgent. He won't mind the
interruption, believe me."

I gave her the number of the pay phone. She
repeated the message back to me. If she was
curious, it didn't show. "And what is your
name?" she asked.

"Just give him the message," I said curtly,
and hung up.

It was kind of a long shot, but it was worth
a try. If Allred didn't call, it wouldn't necessarily mean anything one way or the other.
He probably wouldn't reply to a crank call if
he didn't know what it was about. On the
other hand, he also might just be extremely
cautious. If he did call, he might not say anything that would do us any good. We would
just have to wait and see.

Nothing happened for about five minutes.
"It's not going to work," Dave said.

Before I could answer, the phone rang. I
smiled at Dave and let it ring twice before
picking it up. I held the receiver so Dave could
hear and didn't say anything. There was a few

moments' silence. Then the voice on the other end said, cautiously, "Jack?"

It was Allred. I recognized his voice from court. I didn't answer, just quietly replaced the phone on the hook. That one word, "Jack," told us everything. Dave whistled softly. "Son of a bitch," he said. "I don't believe it."

"Believe it. The question is, now what do we do?"

"You're the guy with the bright ideas."

"Yeah, but it's your turn."

Dave rubbed his forehead. "Fuck, I don't know. Maybe we can get some kind of line on this girl, Julie. She's the only one—" He broke off and stared at me. I got it about the same time he did.

"Jesus," said David, hitting his forehead with his hand. "How could we be so stupid?"

"We're just a couple of regular Sherlock Holmeses."

"Julie."

"Julie," I agreed, disgusted.

"Julie said to stay cool. Julian P. Allred. Juley."

"I won't tell anyone if you won't."

"Juley," Dave muttered, still annoyed with himself. "Jesus."

An hour later we were sitting in an air-conditioned booth at Denny's. Dave stirred the glass of iced tea in front of him with a long spoon, nervously wadding up and then shredding the paper napkins on the table in front of him.

"I still can't quite buy it," he said. "Not totally. I mean, he obviously knows about it, but actually taking part in it? I just don't know, Jase."

" 'Can you believe it?' " I quoted. " 'His own fuckin' lawyer was with him.' "

"Yeah, I know, I know. Biker talk."

"Tell you what," I said, tired of going around and around with it. "What say we find out a little something about what he's been up to lately. Girlfriends, where he hangs out, shit like that."

"That could take a while."

"Well . . ."

"Not another shortcut?" Dave said, wincing. "Jase, have you ever thought about just trying some straight investigative work for once?"

"You want more dead girls while we dig in the files?"

"Yeah, that's what I live for. Lighten up, Jase."

"Okay, sorry. I just thought we might at least talk with someone who knows him a little."

"You got someone in mind?"

"Billy Squires," I said.

Dave thought a moment. "I don't think I know him."

"Dope dealer. I took him down a few years back when I was working narcs. Allred defended him. Got him off with five years."

"Five years? For dope? And I thought Allred was a lawyer."

"Five years' probation. No jail time."

"Oh. Black guy?"

"White. Tall, bushy mustache. Hangs with the ladies a lot. He works for Allred now. Researcher, gofer, that sort of thing. Makes a lot of trips back and forth from the prison."

Dave nodded. "One of those. What makes you think he'd want to talk to us?"

"Oh, you never know. Maybe he will, maybe not. We'll just have to play it by ear. Hey, it can't hurt."

"Okay," Dave said. "Why not?"

Squires lived on the top floor of one of the expensive condo buildings downtown— swimming pool, sauna, hot tubs—all the necessities. We waited until another tenant came out of the lobby and slipped past him, taking the elevator to the top floor. There was no answer when we knocked at the door to his apartment, but when the elevator doors opened to take us back down, Squires almost bumped into us getting off. He glanced at us and then did a double take when he recognized me.

"Coulter," he said. "And here to see me, I'll bet."

"Why do you say that, Billy? Done something lately you shouldn't have?"

"What do you want?"

"Nothing in particular. Just a social visit."

"Right."

"You going to invite us in?"

Billy hesitated, cautious. He knew I wasn't working dope anymore, so he couldn't figure what I was doing there. Curiosity finally got the better of him. "Sure, why not," he said, and led the way down the hall.

Inside the apartment was an immense rug, Persian or Indian, and two leather couches with a steel-and-marble coffee table between them. A twenty-seven-inch Sony sat next to an expensive stereo system. Whatever he was into, Billy was doing all right for himself. We sat down on the couch facing the window, and Billy eased himself onto the other one. He pulled out a cigarette, lit it, and waited for us to say something. We stared back and waited for him to say something. Same old cop games. Finally he gave up on trying to wait us out.

"So what's on your mind?" he asked.

"What are you doing for money these days, Billy?" I asked him.

"Working. I work for Julian Allred. You know that."

"You like it?"

"It's all right."

"I hear he can be a little hard to work for."

Billy shrugged. "He's okay."

"Is he?"

"Yeah. He's an okay guy."

"You ever talk to him about stuff?" Dave put in. "I mean, besides about work?"

"What's this all about, anyway?" Billy asked, crossing his legs. "You got something on Allred?" As soon as he saw we were interested in Allred, not him, he was suddenly a lot more relaxed.

"Just wondering what he's like. Who he hangs with. Stuff like that."

"Why don't you ask him?"

"We thought we'd ask you," Dave said. I waited a couple of beats and added, "We're working homicide these days, Billy."

Billy got that look in his eyes that says, "Forget it. I'm not getting involved."

"I don't really know him all that well," he

said. "I just work for the guy, you know?" He took another drag on his cigarette.

I could see this wasn't going anywhere. I stood up and stretched.

"Well," I said, "we just thought maybe you could help us fill in a few details, but I guess not, so we'll be on our way. You mind if I use your bathroom first?"

"Sure," he said, glad to get rid of us now that he knew we weren't any threat. "Go ahead. Down the hall to your left."

As soon as I closed the bathroom door behind me, I opened the medicine cabinet over the sink. I didn't expect to find anything, but you never know. Maybe some mislabeled prescription drugs. It wouldn't be much of a wedge, but any little thing might help open him up.

The cabinet was full of junk: old Bic razors, half-full cans of shaving cream, toothpaste, nose drops, unidentifiable creams, and a box of baking soda. I tasted it hopefully. Baking soda it was. I started to swing the cabinet mirror back, then smiled as an idea struck me.

In my right jacket pocket were half a dozen small evidence baggies. You never know when you'll need them for saving pieces of evidence, like shell casings. They're the type coin dealers use. Coke dealers use them, too. I filled them quickly from the box of baking soda and sealed them shut.

When I walked back into the living room, Dave was talking, still trying to draw Billy out. I stood between them, opened my hand and let the baggies drop out onto the coffee table.

"Look what I found in the bathroom," I said.

Billy came unglued, leaping to his feet, almost frothing. "You motherfucker!" he howled. "Why, you lying bastard! There's no dope in this house and you know it. Why, you lying motherfucker!"

Hell hath no fury like a dope dealer who really has been set up for once in his life. You'd think that, for someone who believed all cops were dirty anyway, he would have taken it a little more calmly.

"Same old song," I said wearily, looking over at Dave. "Nobody's ever dirty. It's always a setup."

Dave glanced back at me, and I could see he didn't like it. He didn't say anything, though.

"Take it easy, Billy," I said. "I don't work dope anymore, you know that. I don't even care about this shit, you know what I mean?"

Billy sat back down, a disgusted look of comprehension on his face. "You motherfucker," he said again.

I sat down facing him. "Tell me something, Billy. How come a lawyer like Allred spends so much time hanging around with bikers?"

"Fuck you, Coulter," he said. I didn't answer, just reached over and pushed the baggies on the table idly around. He looked at them lying there and looked at me. Finally he leaned back and lit another cigarette.

"Why do you think?" he said. "Chicks. Ladies. Snatch. Why else?"

"He can't get his own?" Dave asked.

Billy smirked at him. "Not fourteen-year-old pussy, he can't. The bikers pick 'em up off the street, runaways, street kids. They take them down to the clubhouse, beat the shit out of them and break them in. They're for, you know, like general consumption. You know what the bikers call them?"

I nodded. "House mice."

"Yeah, right. House mice. So after a week or month or whatever, the bikers kick them out and get in fresh blood. Allred gets his pick then."

"And what do the bikers get out of it?"

"Favors. Legal help. Whatever."

"What happens to the girls after Allred's done with them?" Dave asked.

Billy shrugged. "Back to the street, I guess. You tell me."

I leaned back and stared at the ceiling. Allred was beginning to look better and better.

"You know Jack Holzer?" I asked.

Billy started playing with the cigarette in his hand. "Yeah, I know him. I know who he is."

"Tell me something about him."

Billy shook his head. "He's not the kind of guy you really want to talk about," he said. "Things get around. I don't know that much about him anyway, honest."

"You never seen him with Allred?"

"A couple of times."

"Doing what?"

"I don't know. Holzer comes by the office every once in a while. Sometimes Allred leaves with him."

Billy leaned over the table toward the ashtray to flick in ash. Abruptly he dropped the cigarette and with one wild scoop gathered up the baggies from the table and sprinted toward the bathroom. Dave started after him by reflex, but I grabbed him by the arm and shook me head.

"Time to go," I told him. "We're not going to get any more out of him anyway."

Billy came back out of the bathroom as we were stepping through the door into the hall. His face had a baffled look. He had expected us to be right on his tail when he tried to flush the dope.

"Thanks for the help," I called over my shoulder. "Oh, by the way, you ought to replace the baking soda in your medicine cabinet. It's getting low." I closed the door, and a second later heard an outraged scream of, "Fuck!" from the apartment, followed by a stream of inarticulate curses. I looked at Dave and shrugged. He didn't say anything to me until we were back on the street.

"I wish you wouldn't do things like that, Jason," he said as we got into the car. "One of these days you're going to get us both in a shitload of trouble."

"No evidence, partner. The perpetrator flushed it all down the toilet. Besides, we got what we came for. You still think Allred is just legal counsel?"

"That's not the point."

"That's exactly the point."

Dave sighed. "I just wish you wouldn't do things like that."

Jennifer was just going out the door when I got home. She gave me a quick kiss on the cheek.

"I'm late again," she said, pulling me back down the walkway toward her VW.

"How late will you be back?"

"Nine, maybe ten. Are you going to be home?"

"I hope so. I thought I'd take a nap so I could be a little more awake when you get here."

"That would be nice," she said, getting into the car, leaving the door open to talk. "Whenever I get through with a rehearsal I'm totally wound up. I need to sit and talk for a while to unwind or I can't ever get to sleep."

"Great. We can talk. Or something."

" 'Something' sounds even better. Listen, I've got a free day tomorrow. Is there any way you could get some time off?"

"I doubt it. What did you have in mind?"

"I thought we could go to the zoo."

"The zoo?"

"Yeah. You know, the place where they keep the animals?"

"Oh, the zoo. Why didn't you say so? I don't think so, Jennifer. We're getting close on this case. Next week, maybe."

"Promise?"

"Promise."

The car door slammed and she took off down the street, giving me a little wave as she left. I stood in the driveway and watched until the car turned a corner. I felt absurdly proud of myself. "Ain't love grand," I muttered to myself, half derisively.

I was too tired to even fix anything to eat. I threw myself down on the couch and relaxed for the first time that day. I must have closed my eyes for just a minute. The next thing I knew, the phone was ringing. It was nearly full dark out, and I saw it was almost nine when I glanced over at the clock on the bookshelf. I stumbled over to the phone and picked up the receiver.

"Jason, it's me. We've got another one."

"Who is me?" I asked, still a little disoriented. Falling asleep in the afternoon always does that to me.

"Me. Dave. We've got something, and I think you'd better come down here."

"Here where? Got what?"

"City Creek Canyon, about halfway up."

I was wide-awake now. "Another girl?"

"Just get down here."

"Any witnesses?"

"Not so far."

Dave sounded upset. It took a lot to throw him, so whatever it was, it was bad. I splashed some water on my face, looked longingly at the coffee maker, and decided I'd better pass and get out there as soon as I could and find out what was going on. Maybe I could get one of the patrolmen on the scene to sneak off and get me a cup.

I was pissed at myself. I should have been out working, not home crashed out on the couch. I couldn't believe it was Holzer and friends, though, not so soon after the other one. Nobody could be that far out of control.

City Creek Canyon cuts away north from the city. There are houses right at the bottom, but the rest of it is kept undeveloped. It's a favorite spot for picnics, families, and lovers. At night it's a favorite spot for less wholesome types. About halfway up the canyon I could see a couple of uniformed cars with their overheads flashing, spotlights focused toward an area off the road. Dave's car was pulled over on the shoulder, but he was nowhere in sight. One of the uniformed cops, Frank Waters, greeted me as I stepped out of my car.

"What have we got here, Frank?" I asked as he came up.

"Nothing good, I'm afraid. I was just going up City Creek to check out the summit when I noticed this little VW off the side of the road. Looked like it had run into the ditch, but one of the doors was still open. I stopped, and there was no one in the car, but right by the door there was a purse lying on the ground, stuff spilled all over. We're beating the bushes to see if we can find the lady that goes with it."

When I heard "VW," my throat went dry. "What color is it?" I asked.

Frank looked at me in puzzlement. "The purse?"

"No, the car."

"Oh. Red, a little beat-up. Why?"

The blood started throbbing in my ears. It had to be coincidence.

"Where's the car?" I asked, ignoring his question.

"Over here," he said, leading the way toward a clump of bushes at the side of the road. I could see the back end of the VW, tilted slightly up. The front wheels rested in a ditch. It was Jennifer's car. Her purse was tumbled on the ground by the front door. I looked closely. There was blood on it. Waters continued on blithely, unaware of my reaction.

"I didn't want to touch the purse until the lab guys got here, but I ran a twenty-eight on the car. Belongs to a Jennifer Lassen. I thought . . ." He trailed off as he noticed that I was walking away without listening. Dave came up from a gully behind where the car was, puffing slightly.

"Find anything?" I asked, my voice sounding thin and faraway in my ears.

He shook his head. "There's a running shoe under one of the bushes, but it's old and looks like a man's shoe anyway. I don't think it has anything to do with this." He looked at me sharply. "You okay, Jason?"

"No, I'm not."

"Yeah, it's kind of a shock when . . . wait a minute. Did you two have something going? Oh, my God, you did, didn't you? Oh, Jase, I am sorry."

"I am too."

"It might be okay. She's not here. Something happened, but we don't know what. She could be all right."

"Sure."

Frank Waters interrupted by coming with a tall, gangly kid in tow. "Hey, guys. This kid here thinks he might have seen something."

The kid looked around curiously, hoping maybe to see a body. "Did somebody get killed or something?" he asked.

"Not that we know of," said Dave. "Did you see anything?"

"Well, no, not really. I mean, I didn't see anyone or anything like that. But I noticed that VW when I drove up to the top of the canyon. I went up with my girlfriend, we were going to spend the night up there camping, but . . ."

"You noticed the VW," Dave prompted.

"Yeah, I thought it had run off the road or something, and I was thinking about stopping, but there wasn't anyone around, and besides, there was already another car there."

"What kind of car?"

"Well, it wasn't a car, actually. It was a truck, a big pickup." A fist knotted in my stomach. "It was parked right up next to the car."

"Can you remember the color?" Dave asked.

"Sorry, but I didn't really notice. I mean, it was just a car and a truck, you know? I didn't know anything had happened."

"Older or newer model?"

"I don't know. It was just a pickup."

I walked away, leaving Dave to continue the questioning. It didn't seem to matter. I knew who was in the truck. So did Dave. They had done it again. I wondered if she had fought. My words echoed in my head. *"Don't get into the car.* Fight. Scream." A lot of good that would have done her, out in the middle of the deserted canyon. I wondered how long it would take, if she was dead yet, or if she was still alive, still pleading, still hoping beyond hope that they would let her live after they were through. I had a sudden vision of Fat Eddie's gross body covering hers, grunting and thrusting. I stepped behind a bush and vomited until there was nothing left but dry heaves.

Dave was still talking to the kid. "I'm going home," I told him. He started to say something and then changed his mind.

"I'll keep you posted," he said.

"Yeah, you do that."

When I got home, it was hard. All of Jennifer's stuff was still there. She had been in the house only a couple of days, but it already felt like there was a woman living there. Her leather coat, useless in the heat, was thrown over the back of a chair. Two dance books were lying on the table in the living room. The fan in the bedroom was whirring where she had left it. Her coffee mug was still on the kitchen table, half full. I rinsed it out mechanically and set it in the dish rack. In the bathroom there was dance stuff slung over the shower rod, drying. I thought with a pang that I wasn't going to be able to complain about it now. I took it down and stood there stupidly, my hands full of damp tights. I finally tossed them back over the curtain. On the sink, in a cup, there were two toothbrushes. The cold dread feeling in my stomach expanded into my throat. I was numb. I couldn't swallow, and it felt like I couldn't breathe.

I wandered around the house aimlessly and after a while sat down heavily on the living room couch. I wasn't feeling very good. Up to now I had pretty much been in shock, but it was starting to hit me, really hit me. Rage and grief struggled for dominance. What the hell had she been doing there, anyway, halfway up the canyon? Why had she stopped there? Why did this have to happen? Why the hell did it have to happen to *me?*

I realized what I had just thought. It had happened to her, not me. It was an insight into my own character that I didn't want to deal with, especially now.

The awareness crept up on me slowly. I wasn't going to be seeing Jennifer anymore. We weren't going to be doing things together, after all. We weren't going to be curling up on the couch to watch the late movie. We weren't going to be cheering the Knicks and hissing the Celtics. We weren't going to be bickering over whose turn it was to do the dishes. We weren't going to be doing anything. I wasn't ever going to sleep with her again. I wouldn't feel her lying next to me or hold her as she arched her body next to mine. Never. Not ever.

A small furry head banging against my knee brought me out of it. Stony was looking for his breakfast. He had already accepted Jennifer as part of the household and would be wondering where she was. Not for long, though. A few years ago a battered stray that I named The Rabbit had moved in. After a few months he developed stomach cancer and had to be put to sleep, or, as I used to say, taken to the snuff factory. I had grown quite fond of him and hated to see him go. He had grown so trusting that he sat there quietly while the vet shaved his front paw and slipped in the I.V. with the Pentothal. He looked up at me with those little kitty eyes and started to purr. I think it was the purr that got to me. I'd seen a lot of people on the street die and didn't feel nearly as bad about them as I did about the cat. Then again, I didn't know them nearly as well.

For the first few days after that, Stony kept

looking for The Rabbit to come home. After a week, he had forgotten all about him. That's they way cats are. Jennifer wouldn't be coming home anymore either. It had been a nice visit, but now it was just me and Stony again, the two survivors. I got up and opened a can of cat food and watched him as he ate. Then I sat back down and cried my heart out.

SIX

Professionalism is a word that's used all the time. In one sense it simply means achieving a certain level of competence. In police work it usually means not letting your emotions and personal prejudices get in the way of doing your job.

Over the weekend I was definitely not a professional. I didn't go near the office. I didn't get in touch with Volter. I didn't even call Dave, and I unplugged my phone. I spent most of the time in Little Cottonwood Canyon, south and east of the city.

I'd spent a lot of time in the canyon over the years. I'd done a lot of rock climbing in years past with a girl who talked me into trying it. The climbing faces are always crowded, and in the winter the whole canyon is packed with skiers, but in the summer months, especially up higher, it's a lot less frantic. Ten years ago hardly a soul remained behind when the snow finally melted, and even now, at least up high, the canyon is nearly deserted. On all but the hottest summer days the air is pleasantly cool, as pure with the scent of spruce and fir as a hundred years ago. It is timeless country; year follows year, season follows season, the snows come and go, birds dart from the shelter of one tree to another, furry ground squirrels scramble in the sparse cover, and red-tailed hawks glide through the summer sky. I wandered the high places and walked through some of the most peaceful country on earth with only one thought. Revenge.

Jennifer was dead, her body dumped God knows where. I had hardly even known her, but there was still overwhelming rage. They had taken her away in their pickup, amused themselves, and then taken her life. They had taken something from me as well. Perhaps things between us wouldn't have worked out. She might well have simply faded from my life. Or maybe she really was the one, the woman who would have become my life and love. I would never know. I would never have the chance to find out. There was nothing I could do about it, and there was no point in crying out, "It isn't fair." Things seldom are. But they weren't going to get away with it. Not this time. One way or another, they were going to pay.

"Where the hell have you been?" were the first words out of Mike Volter's mouth when I walked into the office Monday morning.

"Don't start with me, Mike," I cautioned, sitting down at my desk. He followed me there and stood over me.

"All right, Jason," he said in a milder tone. "Dave told me that you were close to the girl killed up in City Creek, Jennifer Larson."

"Lassen," I corrected automatically.

"Sorry. Lassen. I know how you must feel, but you can't just take off like that because you're upset. We've got a job to do. There are a lot of things to check out, a lot of stuff that has to be done."

I looked up at him. "Mike," I said levelly, "drop it. Just drop it." I thought for a moment he was going to push it, but he thought better of it. "Any sign of her body turn up?" I asked.

"Sorry, Jason, not yet." He shook his head. "Most of these women, we never are going to find them, you know."

"Yeah," I said. "I know." I looked around the office. "Has Dave been in yet?"

"He's down at arraignment court. The county picked up Edward Wrones last night." He paused. "We tried to get hold of you," he said pointedly. I looked at him blankly.

"The guy they call Fat Eddie," he explained. "Hal Webster got him I.D.'ed from a photo spread." I was out the door almost before he finished his sentence, and five minutes later I was talking to Dave on the fifth floor of the Courts Building. Dave tactfully didn't mention anything about my little disappearing act over the weekend.

"I guess you heard they picked up Fat Eddie, then," he said as I came up.

"Volter kindly mentioned it to me. I thought I'd stop by and take a look at him."

"A look is about all we're going to get. You'll never guess who's representing him. You get three tries and the first two don't count."

"Speak of the devil," I said, as Allred walked up, squeezing by us to enter the courtroom. He gave us a friendly nod as he passed, counselor to detective, on opposite sides, maybe, but still part of the vast law enforcement fraternity. As always, dapper and professional. Dark blue three-piece suit. Dark hair, wavy, fashionably graying at the temples, carefully styled and blow-dried. He was about forty, looked older, and projected an air of quiet competence. He had a real courtroom presence. He actually brushed against my arm as he went through the door. It felt like a snake had slithered across it.

"Surprise, surprise," said Dave.

"Yeah," I said. "I don't suppose by any chance he let you talk to Fat Eddie?"

"Oh, I talked to him all right. Me and Hal Webster. We didn't get a thing. Not a word. Allred told him to keep his mouth shut, and that's exactly what he's doing."

"That's going to make it tough."

"Tell me about it." Dave spoke casually, but his eyes showed anger.

Inside the courtroom, we sat down in the back row of spectator's seats. Allred was already seated at the defense table, whispering something in the ear of another defense attorney. There were a lot of people in arraignment court, mostly wives, girlfriends, and assorted relatives of people who had been picked up over the weekend.

Names were being called in alphabetical order, so we had a while to wait before Fat Eddie's case came up. I looked around the courtroom, and on the other side of the room I saw Jack Holzer. I couldn't believe it. This was the first time I had seen him in the flesh, but I recognized him instantly from his mug shot. He was wearing a blue Levi's jacket and jeans, and seemed totally at ease. One foot, showing a worn cowboy boot, was propped negligently on the seat in front of him, while the other sprawled out in the aisle.

There wasn't much to him at first look. Medium size, medium weight, regular features, sandy hair cut medium short—just your typical average guy. He didn't look like a biker. No earrings, no tattoos that I could see, nothing that indicated that he was anything more than an ordinary guy going about ordinary business. I prodded Dave and gestured with my head.

"Holzer," I mouthed. He followed my glance across the room.

"Well, I'll be damned," he muttered. "Talk about nerve."

"Why not? There isn't any way we can make a case on him."

"Not yet. Maybe you and I should have a little talk with Mr. Holzer after court."

Holzer was leaning back in his seat, scanning the faces around the courtroom, unaware of our scrutiny. Our eyes met for a second. He had no idea who I was. He didn't appear particularly weird or crazy, but he was still scary. His eyes went right through to the back of his head, and there was nothing inside. No hate, no anger, certainly no fear. Nothing but a cold watchfulness, dark, empty, compassionless, and as unconcerned with human feelings as the bright and glittering eyes of a chicken.

I told myself I was seeing more in him than was really there. I knew what he was. I knew the things he had done. To anyone else, his eyes were probably quite ordinary, just like the rest of him. Dave leaned over toward me.

"That is one very cold dude," he whispered. "Look at his eyes. They watch, but there's nobody home."

So maybe they weren't so ordinary after all.

Judge Burton took the bench and the parade of humanity started through. One by one they approached and spoke their piece. Marston, Public Intox. Not guilty, Your Honor. Bail set at fifty dollars. Rodriguez, Burglary. Not guilty, Your Honor. Can you afford an attorney? No, Your Honor. See the clerk. The legal defender's office will assign you one. Bail is set at fifteen hundred dollars. Thank you, Your Honor. Wilson, Soliciting Sex Acts. Not guilty, Your Honor. Bail is set at one hundred dollars. The bureaucracy of justice rolled smoothly along.

Finally the jailer brought Fat Eddie out from the holding cell. The man was simply enormous. He was well over six feet, and must have run close to three hundred fifty pounds. If Holzer didn't fit the standard image of a biker, Fat Eddie certainly did. He was dressed in a dirty white T-shirt and baggy Levi's that kept slipping down, threatening to expose the crack of his massive buttocks. Every few seconds he would hitch them back up into place, only to have them slip back down again. Tattoos covered both arms. Jet-black hair, tangled and matted, reached down to his shoulders. His teeth were stained and rotten, and little button eyes peered out from a full bushy beard covering his entire face. What little face could be seen under the beard was acne-scarred and greasy, with a repulsive, soft, doughy look. He resembled nothing so much as a giant, hairy Pillsbury Dough-Boy, horribly transformed into some grotesque monster by a child's fearful dream. An ancient scar, barely visible, ran down the right side of his neck from just below the ear to the shoulder blade. He stood there malevolently, every mother's nightmare, a walking affront to civilized society, and he reveled in it.

"Wrones, Edward C." intoned the bailiff. "Attempted Kidnapping; Criminal Homicide, Murder First Degree; Parole Violation."

The bailiff read the charges with no more inflection than he had for the cases of Public Intoxication. Allred got up from the attorney's table and approached the bench.

"Your Honor, I am representing Mr. Wrones in this matter," he stated. "Mr. Wrones wishes to enter a plea of not guilty to all charges." The judge made a notation on his pad and looked down at the copy he held of the arrest warrant.

"It states here that Mr. Wrones is presently on parole from Utah State Prison." he said. "Is that information correct, Mr. Wrones?" Fat Eddie turned his head toward Allred.

"Yes, Your Honor," Allred conceded. "That is correct."

"The complaint also alleges he was carrying a firearm at the time of his arrest, in violation of the terms of his parole. Any comment, Mr. Allred?"

"None at this time, Your Honor."

I looked a question at Dave. "Just a .22 derringer," he whispered. "Not the murder weapon."

"Mr. Wrones will remain in custody without bail on a parole hold until the preliminary hearing," Judge Burton continued. "The first day I have open is two weeks from this Tuesday, July 25. Is that agreeable to you, Mr. Allred?"

"Yes, Your Honor."

"Mr. Feison?"

"Yes, Your Honor," said the prosecutor, rising from his table. The judge made some more notes on his calendar and handed a sheaf of papers to the court clerk. Fat Eddie was led away after a few words with Allred, and the next case was called.

As soon as Fat Eddie was gone, Holzer got to his feet and left the courtroom. Dave and I followed him out.

"How about letting me do the talking?" Dave said to me as we walked down the hallway.

"Why?" I asked. "You think I can't handle it?"

"You're a little close to this one, Jase."

"So are you."

"Not in quite the same way."

I shrugged my acceptance.

We caught up with Holzer right around the corner as he stood waiting for the elevator. He turned those flat eyes on us as we approached.

"You Jack Holzer?" Dave asked.

Holzer studied him carefully before answering.

"Who wants to know?" he finally replied. He spoke with a slight trace of the South in his speech, Texas, maybe. Dave showed him his shield.

"Detective Warren, Salt Lake City Police." He motioned toward me. "Detective Coulter."

Holzer leaned nonchalantly back against the wall. "City guys," he said lazily. "Well, well. And just what can I do for you fellows today?"

"Nothing much. We'd just kind of like to ask you about a couple of things."

"Like what?"

"Just some things. You willing to answer some questions?"

"It depends."

"On what?"

"On the questions."

Holzer was sparring with us, actually enjoying himself, which was fine. You can get a lot of information from someone who thinks they're clever enough to play verbal games with the cops. Before Dave could go any further, though, there was an interruption. Allred turned the corner, saw us with Holzer, and immediately strode up, a big smile creasing his face.

"Well, gentleman, and what have we got here?" he inquired, the soul of affability.

"Nothing that concerns you, counselor," I said, before Dave had a chance to speak. "That is, unless Mr. Holzer here is your client." I gave him a cold stare. "Is he?"

I was trying to present Allred with a small problem. He didn't like the idea that we were talking to Holzer, but he also wouldn't be any too anxious to connect himself with Holzer until he had time to think over all the angles. Especially after that phone call I'd made. It didn't faze him, though.

"Well, no," he said, "I'm not actually representing him at the moment, but I have done so in the past. And being acquainted with Mr. Holzer, I feel it incumbent on me to offer legal assistance if I can be of service."

Holzer grinned at him. "Sure," he said. "Stick around, Juley."

Allred was visibly annoyed at the familiar tone, but he didn't say anything about it.

"Is Mr. Holzer a suspect in some crime?" he asked.

"Not officially, no."

"Unofficially, then?"

"We just have a few question we'd like to ask."

"Concerning what?"

Dave smiled at him nastily. "Rape and murder. Little things like that."

Allred didn't blink an eye. "Those are very serious charges," he said.

"Yes, I'm aware of that," Dave said dryly. "That's why I want to ask some questions."

"Well, I'm not sure that under these circumstances I could advise my client—"

"Oh, he's your client now," I broke in.

"Speaking on a temporary basis—"

I looked over at Dave, and he nodded. There wasn't much point in continuing. Allred wasn't going to let Holzer say anything that would be of any help, and any questions we posed would only give them information about how much we knew.

The elevator dinged its arrival, and we stepped into the car, leaving Allred in midsentence. I caught the door, just as it was about to close, and leaned out.

"See you around, Jack," I said, unable to keep the hatred out of my voice. "Soon. You too, counselor . . . Juley."

Connie Alter, one of the records clerks, was already in the elevator when we got on. She looked at us with curiosity.

"I see you know Jack Holzer," she said.

Dave sighed. "Looks like everybody knows him but us."

"Oh, I don't really know him. You know Marsha, in dispatch? She pointed him out to me once when we were at Santa's Saloon."

"I didn't know you went to places like that, Connie," I said.

She smiled archly. "There's a lot of things about me you don't know."

"Yeah, I'll bet," said Dave.

"How does Marsha know him?" I asked.

"She used to go out with one of the Pharaohs. That's before she came to work here," Connie hurriedly added.

"Marsha? Come on."

"No, really. She used to be a little wild. She doesn't do any of that stuff anymore."

"I'll bet," said Dave again.

"She doesn't. Anyway, she doesn't actually know him. She just pointed him out and told me never to even talk to him. He's some kind of weirdo or something."

"So it seems," I agreed.

"Yeah. I guess there are all kinds of stories about him. She heard he had this party once, and had a giant punchbowl in his backyard, with these huge chunks of ice floating around in it, and frozen in each chunk was a tiny little kitten."

"Meow," said Dave.

"Don't," said Connie. "That's awful. What's he done, anyway?"

"Good question," I said.

Mike Volter was still at the office when we got back, and the first thing he did was to take me aside for a talk. He sat down across from me and put on his best fatherly tone. At any other time I would have been amused.

"Jason," he said, a concerned look on his face, "you're much too close to this case. I don't think you should be working it. Maybe you ought to back off and let someone else handle it."

What I should have done was just play it cool and reassure him I was in control, but I couldn't be bothered with that kind of crap right now. I had too much else to think about.

"Mike, I'm not dropping this case," I told him. "Forget it. Not a chance." Of course, that was the exact wrong tack. It was a challenge, and he had to respond.

"That's just the sort of thing I'm talking about, Jason. Your emotions are running away with you. You've lost your objectivity, and when you—"

"Bullshit," I interrupted.

"You don't leave me much choice, with that attitude."

"So?"

"So starting as of right now, you're back on regular duty. Leave this case alone. I'm going to put someone else on it with Dave."

I was almost speechless, but not quite.

"Fuck you, Mike," I said, spun around, and walked out the door.

"Jason, get back in here!" he yelled at my back. I turned partially, gave him the finger, and kept on walking. It was a choice of that or getting into real trouble. If I had come back, I would have decked him. Mike didn't follow me out. At least he had that much sense.

After driving around aimlessly for a while, I'd managed to calm down enough to go home. There was one simple and inescapable fact: If I wanted back in on the case, I had some fences to mend. I knew Mike Volter pretty well and how his mind worked. If I went in tomorrow, serious and contrite, I could probably get him to put me back on the case. Even if he didn't, I could get Dave to feed me information and work it on my own time. But if I wasn't careful, I could end up getting suspended and watching the whole thing from the sidelines. And that, of all things, I could not tolerate.

SEVEN

Mike's reaction was pretty much along the lines I had figured. After making me eat dirt for a while, he loosened up and let me back in. He was also counting on Dave to keep an eye on me, which was a laugh. I'd pulled Dave out of at least as many scrapes as he had me.

It was a good thing I had patched things up with Mike, though. There was a lineup scheduled that afternoon with Fat Eddie, and I wanted to be there. The witness from the Pay-Less on State Street had already identified him from pictures, but in a capital case, a lineup I.D. is mandatory. I didn't figure he'd have a whole lot of trouble picking him out. Fat Eddie wasn't someone you forgot easily. I did wonder where five other people who even remotely resembled him were going to come from, but Mike said they had managed.

Allred was waiting in the lineup room, along with George Feison, the prosecutor; our witness; Hal Webster and another guy from the county; Dave; and myself. Feison was giving his usual spiel to the witness about how the glass was one way, how the suspect couldn't see in, and how everything was perfectly safe. I wondered if it occurred to the poor guy that sooner or later he was going to have to get up on the witness stand, look right into Fat Eddie's beady eyes, and point the finger. I just hoped he wouldn't realize that quite yet. Thoughts like those tend to impair the memory.

The door behind the glass opened, and the lineup suspects trooped in. I recognized one of them as a guy who worked down at the city shops as a mechanic. Fat Eddie was fourth from the right, and stood out like a hippopotamus in a herd of cows. They had done their best, but there just wasn't anyone around who came close to him. Allred was busy taking notes. He would be sure to mention that fact in court. Our witness whispered something to George Feison, who leaned toward the microphone.

"Will you all please turn to the right?" he said. Six figures did so in unison, an elephant drill team. "Now left, please. Face front again." There was another whispered conference. "Number Six, will you step forward?" Number Six was the largest man there, except for Fat Eddie. "Thank you. Step back. Number Two, step forward, please."

Dave turned to me with a look that said, "what the hell is going on?" There wasn't any way our guy didn't recognize Fat Eddie. I shrugged and looked over at where he was seated behind the viewing table. There was a film of perspiration on his lip, and he looked nervous. Everyone trying to identify suspects from a lineup is nervous, but he looked worse than usual. Allred was looking over at him with a faint suggestion of a smile on his face. I suddenly caught on.

"That's all, gentlemen," said Feison, and the suspects filed back out the door. Allred closed his notebook with a snap.

"So, George," he said, "it didn't look to me like there was any identification."

"Well, he's not absolutely sure. He wants to think about it."

"Not sure? It's kind of difficult to convict when you're 'not sure,' don't you think?"

Feison sighed. The case had just gone down the toilet, but he wasn't going to admit it to Allred until he had to. "We'll manage," he said shortly. Allred nodded condescendingly, gathered his stuff, and walked out. He hadn't even glanced at Dave or me the whole time. George Feison looked over at us and spread his hands. "Sorry," he said. "We tried."

"I'm sorry too," said the witness. "I wish I could have been more help. When I actually saw them all standing there, I just couldn't be positive. I wanted to, but I simply couldn't be sure."

"That's okay," said Feison. "You did your best." Dave let out a snort of disgust behind me. Feison walked out the door with the witness. Hal Webster stared after them, pulling on his tie.

"Goddamned son of a bitch," he spat. "Too scared to say a word."

"You think someone got to him?" asked Dave.

"What, are you kidding me? What do you think? And who the fuck cares, anyway? Now the whole case is totally screwed. If he gets brave and changes his mind, so what? That asshole Allred will tear him apart on the stand. Now it's back to square one. Jesus fucking Christ." He stormed out of the room and slammed the door behind him.

"That man is angry," said Dave.

"Yeah. I noticed. I'm not exactly bubbling over myself."

"Me either. What say we talk to our witness?"

"Let me. Both of us together will just scare him worse."

"Whatever you think. I'll be back at the office."

I caught up with them outside in the courtyard just as Feison was shaking hands goodbye. Our witness saw me coming and set his face in a determined look. I put out my hand as I walked up.

"I don't think we've actually met," I said. "Jason Coulter. I'm working on this case."

"Bill Hunt," he said, taking my hand. "I'm really sorry I couldn't be sure about that guy. I thought I could identify him, but they all looked so much alike." That was a joke if ever I'd heard one. I took a soothing tone.

"Yeah, I know, it can be difficult sometimes.

Making an I.D. isn't as easy as people think."
He jumped on it eagerly.

"No, it isn't, it really isn't."

"Well, we appreciate the effort. How old are you, Bill?" He looked puzzled.

"Twenty-seven. Why?"

"Married?"

"Yes."

"Kids?"

"Four." Four kids at twenty-seven meant that he was almost certainly Mormon.

"Did you ask your bishop what you should do in a case like this?"

He started to look a little wary. "A case like what?"

"Like when they came to see you. What, was it at your house or at the store?"

"I'm not entirely sure I know what you're talking about." He looked me right in the eye, but his face started to color and he swallowed convulsively. He wasn't a very good liar. Of course, Mormons aren't supposed to practice that particular art.

"Bill," I said, taking him by the arm and leading him over to a bench in the courtyard, "sit down a minute. We need to talk about this."

"About what?" he asked, speaking too quickly. He was going to play it out as far as he could.

I sat down beside him on the bench, leaned my elbow on my knee, put my chin in my hand, and regarded him steadily. He started to get nervous. "Hey, do you think I'm lying about this or something? Why would I do that?" I kept looking at him. "I want to help, really. Can I help it if—"

"Bullshit," I interrupted. He got huffy and started into his indignant act.

"I don't have to take this, you know. I came down here of my own free will—"

I interrupted again, switching back to soothing. "Listen, I understand. Really, I do. But it's important that I find out who threatened you. You don't have to testify, but it would really help me to know what happened."

He hesitated, and for a moment I thought he was going to level with me. Then his face settled back into a bland puzzlement. They must have really gotten to him.

"I'm sorry," he said, "but I just don't know what you're talking about." He licked his lips and came out with what seemed to be a non sequitur, but I knew better. "I've got kids, you know."

I gave up. There wasn't much point in pursuing it anyway.

Back at the office, Volter was ready, waiting for another explosion, so I just said, "You win some, you lose some," and sat down at my desk. I didn't get much done, though. I just stared out the window.

Now I knew how it felt. "I'm sorry, but there's nothing we can do." I must have spoken that line to victims a hundred times. I'd never fully understood what the look of despair on their faces really meant. I'd thought I did, but I didn't. Fat Eddie. Holzer. Julian P. Fuckin' Lawyer Allred. They were going to walk, and there was nothing anyone could do about it.

I kept looking out the window and seeing Allred's affable smile and Holzer's self-assured smirk. Flashes of Jennifer lying in bed, naked, smiling at me, mixed with images of all the dead women I'd ever seen, hopelessly twisted up together. Then Fat Eddie, gross and repulsive. A couple of times I caught myself whistling tunelessly, a bad habit I'd picked up whenever I was under stress.

I don't know exactly when the idea came to me. It wasn't that clear. It certainly wasn't anything conscious. One moment I was daydreaming; the next I had made a decision.

I quit daydreaming and started to do some serious thinking. One thing was very clear: Whatever else, I was *not* prepared to pay the consequences. Killing someone is not all that difficult; killing a specific person when you have a strong motive and getting away with it is another matter. I had no intention of spending any part of my life at Point of the Mountain, courtesy of the state of Utah.

The immediate problem was Fat Eddie. He wasn't going to take a fall for murder, but he would be going back to prison on a parole violation for carrying that gun. He'd probably be out there for another year, and a lot can happen in a year. I might screw up and be out there with him, and a cop doesn't last very long out at the joint. Worse, I might screw up and get myself killed. Holzer in particular wouldn't be that easy to take down. Fat Eddie would have to go first, and that wouldn't be easy either, since he was going to be behind bars instead of out on the street. It could be done, though. In fact . . .

"Hey, Jason. Planet Earth calling Jason. Come in, Jason." I looked up and saw Dave standing over me.

"Sorry. I was thinking."

"No shit. I'm going for lunch. You coming?"

"Not today. I've got some stuff to do." He peered at me, a worried expression on his face.

"Anything you'd care to talk over with your partner?"

"Not right now, Dave. But thanks."

"Let me know when you're ready," he said, and ambled off toward the elevator.

After a few moments of contemplation I strolled over to Mike Volter's office and rapped on the open door. He looked up from his desk and waved me in.

"Yeah, Jase?"

"Mike, I been thinking about what you said the other day about getting too close to this case, and I think maybe you've got a point. Maybe I ought to take a couple of weeks' vacation time and get all this straightened out in my head."

Mike nodded thoughtfully. With all the work on the floor there was no way he would approve two weeks off ordinarily, but now that I was eating crow and bowing to his superior wisdom, there wasn't any way he could turn it down.

"I think that's a good idea, Jason," he said. "I'm glad to see you're getting things in perspective a little. Maybe you're finally growing up. You going to take a trip, or what?"

"I might go away for a few days. I've got

some friend in Colorado I haven't seen in a while."

"Good idea. Fill out the request form and I'll approve it. When are you thinking of leaving?"

"Couple of days. I've got a few things here to take care of first."

"You'll fill Dave in on anything that needs to be taken care of while you're gone?"

"Sure. There isn't anything immediate, except for this case, and it's not going anywhere. By the way, whatever happened with that girl who got her head caved in on the fireplace? Becker come up with anything on it?"

Becker was walking by and stuck his head in when he heard his name. "You talking about that cute Mexican snatch who died giving a little too much head?"

I didn't answer. I had long ago given up trying to pretend Becker was a human being.

"You can forget that," said Volter. "Her husband came in this morning while you were at the lineup and copped to it. Seems she was seeing another guy on the side and he just lost it. Claims it was an accident, that he just pushed her and she fell into the mantel."

"Right."

"Well, a jury will probably buy it. He'll end up copping to manslaughter."

"Sounds fair. He'll be out in what, a couple of years, maybe three? What the hell, the girl would have been dead in another fifty or sixty years anyway."

"We don't make the rules, Jason."

"Maybe we should."

Volter stared up at me. "You need a vacation," he said.

"So I've been told. See you in a couple of weeks."

As soon as I left the station, I went home and threw a few things in a bag. I left a huge bowl of dry food out for Stony, filled my car up at the local self-service, stopped at the bank for a large wad of cash, and was on the road by late afternoon.

I headed out west past the Great Salt Lake— lately grown a little greater than was comfortable for the residents of the city. In bad weather waves now lapped at the sides of I-80, and every time a storm hit, the road would have to be temporarily closed. I followed I-80 through Wendover, down to Elko, on past Winnemucca, and into Reno, stopping only for gas, and then only at self-service stations, always paying cash. I made good time.

By seven in the morning San Francisco was in view. Crossing over the Bay Bridge and on into the city, I reflected I hadn't been to the Bay Area for quite a while. It used to be my home, but that was more years ago than I care to remember, back in the hippie days. Those were good times. There was good dope. There were great parties. There were a thousand women who wanted to get it on, and the dread word AIDS was not yet part of our common language. Rock 'n' roll had taken over. We were the generation that was going to set the world on its ear. With that awful arrogance of youth, we knew we were different from any generation that had come before. Maybe it was true, but somehow, something went out of us all as the years passed. Maybe it was just that we finally grew up.

Best of all, I was young. No responsibilities, no worries, and certainly no conscience. The late sixties and early seventies were a trip. I feel sorry for the kids today. They have no idea what they missed.

Willard's house was on Caselli Street, a little side street in the middle of the Castro District. Back in the mid seventies, when the neighborhood was still lower middle and working class and rents were still pretty cheap, we shared the house for a couple of years. The house went up for sale, and somehow Willard managed to scrape up enough for a down payment, although his job as a commercial artist wasn't paying him much at the time. Now he's free-lance, one of the best in the city, and charges hefty fees.

He wanted to go in on the house with me, but I had just met a girl from the University of Utah and decided to go back to Salt Lake City with her. The girl lasted only six months, but somehow I never got around to leaving the valley. One day I woke up and realized I had been in Salt Lake for over ten years and that somehow, instead of the carefree bohemian I had always intended to be, I was a cop in a small town grown into a big city.

Driving up Castro Street, I was struck again with what bizarre changes had occurred in the old neighborhood. Gone were the Mom and Pop grocery stores. Chic boutiques alternated with trendy bars, and on every corner a parade of young men in tight jeans swirled by, eyeing each other hopefully. The gay community had taken over with a flourish, and almost no one else could afford to live there anymore.

It was kind of sad to see the old neighborhood transformed into an alien world. I shrugged. There was no point worrying about it. It was good for Willard, though. By now he had paid off his mortgage and had converted the house into two flats. The top one was rented out for an exorbitant price, which his renters were more than willing to pay, while he kept the bottom half with the garden. He had a place to live, in a city that was rapidly becoming unaffordable, and the rent from the upper flat provided him with a very nice source of income.

I parked my car over on 18th Street, the only place I could find, and walked back over to the house. I rang the bell and waited for a while. Willard didn't like getting up early any more than I did, and he was probably figuring that if he ignored the bell, he could get back to sleep. I gave it three more long rings, and finally the door flung open and a very annoyed Willard was standing on the threshold, blinking at me in the morning light. Tall, gaunt, unshaven, and bleary, he was a welcome sight.

"Jason? What in God's name are you doing here?" A thought flashed across his face. "You got trouble?"

"Yes and no. Are you going to invite me in?"

"Oh, yeah, sorry, sorry. Come in, come in."

I laughed. Willard tends to double up on his phrases when he gets flustered. I followed him into the kitchen. I think we spent 90 percent of our time in that room, back in the old days. It was a room with good memories. The big scarred oak table was still in the corner, next to the sliding glass doors that led out to the garden. The old-fashioned gas range was still there too, although there was a new refrigerator humming quietly by the stove. The kitchen shelves were crammed with every type of gadget imaginable for preparing food. Willard fancies himself, among other things, a gourmet chef. He isn't that bad, either.

Just looking around the room made me feel better. We used to sit around the oak table in the evenings, sometimes just the two of us, sometimes with our current female interests, and talk about anything and everything. We would drink cheap wine, and maybe smoke a little of that good northern California dope, and laugh about how good life could be.

Willard started some coffee brewing and sat down across the table.

"So how are things in Salt Lake City?" he asked finally.

"Not so good."

"What's going on?"

"Tell you later."

"Okay. How long are you here for?"

"I'm not sure. I hope just today. I want to pick up a few things here and be on my way."

"What sort of things?"

"Oh, just some things."

"Such as?"

"Maybe a couple of guns."

"Oh. They don't sell guns in Salt Lake?"

"Not guns that can't be traced back to me."

"I see. Do I want to know why you want guns that can't be traced?"

"I don't think so. I don't think you even want to know that I was here."

"I see."

"You said that already."

"I did, didn't I?" He got up and poured two cups of coffee. "You need some help, Jase?"

I smiled. That was Willard all right. No questions asked about what I was doing. Just a casual offer of help.

"Well, yes and no," I replied.

Willard yawned and took a gulp of coffee. "My, aren't we cryptic this morning?"

"Sorry. I've been driving all night. Listen, do they still have that flea market out in Marin?"

"So far as I know."

"Could we run out there this morning?"

"So you can buy a few guns?"

"Sort of. Actually, so you can buy them."

"I don't need any guns."

"I know that."

Willard took another gulp of coffee. "Am I going to end up in the slammer when you screw up?"

"I'm not planning to screw up."

"Well, that's certainly reassuring," he said. He stood up and stretched. "Let me throw some clothes on, then."

EIGHT

As soon as Willard came back to the kitchen, we started out for Marin County.

"My car or yours?" I asked.

"Mine. Host always drives."

I wanted to get there early enough to still have a good choice of items, but late enough to get lost in the crowd of bargain shoppers, so we drove around the city for a while. San Francisco is a fascinating city, a simply astonishing mixture of total opposites. It always amazes me that such a diverse group of people can exist in the same place without being at each other's throats every minute. San Francisco has had its ups and downs over the years, but the basic tenor of the city has never changed—live and let live. It isn't a bad system by which to operate a city. It isn't such a bad system for people, either, come to think of it.

We drove around the edges of the Tenderloin, where the seedy side of town pushes against the up-and-coming chic neighborhoods-to-be. On Powell Street shops that belong in different cities, not just on different streets, nestle incongruously together in uneasy harmony. "Waldo's Cheese Nook" vies for business with the next door "Hard-on Leather for Men." Whips and chains in one window; imported Brie in the next. San Francisco at its finest.

We stopped at a red light, and I heard a staccato tapping coming from the alley off to our left. A stylish woman in a business suit was taking a shortcut through the block. Her high heels struck the cobblestones like tiny hammers, and the sound reverberated off the surrounding buildings, announcing her passage. She stepped briskly along, oblivious to the refuse strewn around the alley, intent on her own world. As she approached the street, a figure stirred itself from the side of the alley. A bum had been sleeping there, newspaper over his face. He sat bolt upright, with as sour an expression as ever I have seen on a human face. He looked around in disgust, saw the woman, and shouted at the top of his voice, "Lady, for Christ's sake, *get some fuckin' rubber heels.*" The paper went back over his face, and he turned away again to the side of the building. Once again San Francisco at its finest.

While we were driving around, I filled Willard in on what was going on. He deserved that much. He had some questions, not on the ethics of the situation, but on the practical aspects.

"You really think you can do this?"

"Oh, yes. I can."

"Without getting yourself killed? These do not sound like pleasant people."

"I'm not feeling too pleasant myself these days."

"What if you get caught?"

"I told you, I'm not planning to get caught."

Willard shook his head mournfully. "Who does?" he muttered.

He was silent for a while.

"What about serial numbers?" he asked suddenly. "Can't they trace a gun that way?"

"Real unlikely. Sure, theoretically it's possible, but the reality is a lot different. I figure the odds of tracing a used firearm from its original source at the factory to a specific vendor at a flea market in California are about a hundred to one against."

"Not bad."

"Also, a lot of the guys who sell stuff at the flea markets roam all over the western states. Most of them have no fondness for law enforcement. The cooperation they give to cops is about zero."

"Well, okay," said Willard. "But why not just file off the serial number and avoid the whole problem?"

"Well, I could, but in order to do that, you have to cut almost all the way into the barrel, and that can weaken it. Even then there's new technology for bringing out obliterated numbers. It's a lot safer not to have to rely on that."

"Interesting."

"What's more, you're the one buying the guns. They wouldn't be showing your picture to the vendors anyway; they'd be showing mine. They don't even know you exist. The chances of connecting it all up are more like a hundred thousand to one."

Willard cursed a driver in a red Fiat who cut in front of us.

"Of course," he said, "I just read in the paper yesterday that the last lottery winner beat odds of ten million to one."

"Well, there you have it. Things like that can't happen twice in a row."

"Thanks. That's very comforting."

"Don't mention it."

About ten we headed out toward Marin. Willard cut down Farrell Street, then out on Lombard toward the Golden Gate Bridge. I noticed that the farther you get from the center of the city, the less individuality San Francisco seems to have. Outer Lombard Street could be anywhere U.S.A. It could be a street in Kansas or Iowa for all the character it shows. Only a quick glimpse of a man carrying a wicker basket and a handful of balloons reminded me that I was still in northern California.

"Entering Marin County," reads a small sign about halfway across the bridge. I didn't notice any sudden change, but Willard told me if I watched carefully I would see a little-known phenomenon occurring. He claimed that as the pedestrians crossed the county line into Marin, the hot dogs they were carrying became magically transformed into sushi. It was a nice thought.

By the time we reached the market, it was packed. Town ordinances prohibit parking on the nearby streets during the weekend, a clever money-making ploy, since there are plenty of lots where the owner is willing to let you park for a couple of bucks. We passed up the two-dollar lot right next to the market and paid a buck to an ancient black gentleman for a space in a field two blocks away. I handed Willard all the cash I had with me. He would be doing all the talking and buying while I was checking out weapons as unobtrusively as possible.

The flea market in Marin County isn't really a market. It's more a gigantic parking lot, jammed with people buying and selling every conceivable type of merchandise. All the vendors operate right out of their vehicles. Some are small time, with little more to offer than a station wagon filled with junk, and only the tailgate for a display table. Others own converted school buses and spread out their merchandise on folding tables around the entire area, jostling for space with their adjacent competition. There must have been five hundred vehicles packed into the lot, and the crowd was so thick that if you got separated from a friend, it would take an hour to find each other again. There were tools, books, cameras, stereos, jewelry, silverware, and clothes. There were comic books and carved ducks. There was one table flanked by two matching elephants, the size of Newfoundlands, carved out of polished black stone. On the table between them was a striking array of miniature curios, including a whole row of hand-carved ivory skulls.

We drifted awhile among the displays, until Willard pulled me by the arm to a table in the center of the lot. A dark-haired man of indeterminate race was trying to sell a young kid a portable radio-cassette player. The boy's father looked on, amused. The boy was trying to listen to the various radios on the table, but they were difficult to hear over the noise of the crowd.

"How much do you want for one of these?" asked the boy hesitantly, gesturing at the table. The man selling the radios smiled at him, putting on his friendliest manner. He was wearing a long-sleeved blue pullover, and he wiped his forehead with one of the sleeves. It was hot in the middle of the lot.

"Tell me which one you want," he said. "Tell me what you're interested in. We'll find a price."

The boy picked up a little silver job and turned it on. It sounded like it was being played underwater.

"Hey, kid, you got really good taste. That's a Sony. The sound is really fine. Check it out. The thing is, it's got one bad battery. You put in another battery and you'll have something. Eight dollars. I can let you have it for eight dollars."

The boy glanced at his father, who looked dubious. The man in the blue pullover started talking to the father.

"Seven dollars. Tell you what, I'll let it go for seven dollars. That's what it cost me. It's a real deal. Check it out."

The boy started pulling on his father's sleeve. The man shrugged good-naturedly and pulled out his wallet.

Willard was interested in the byplay between the man and his customers. I was interested in a .25 auto that lay on the back of the table. I poked Willard. "I want to take a look at that gun," I told him. He nodded and walked up to the table.

"How much for that pistol?" Willard asked the man, pointing to the gun.

"This? That's a fine piece of machinery, buddy. It's a Star, made by the Spanish. They make some very fine weapons."

I'm sure the Spanish make some fine guns, but this was not one of them. I was familiar with the Star, and it was one step up from a Saturday night special. That suited me perfectly. If I used it at all, it was going to be at very close range. It was also going to be a lot harder to trace than a Colt or a Smith & Wesson. In general, the cheaper the weapon, the less likely people are to keep track of it.

Willard looked it over for a minute, and then handed it over to me, distracting the man by asking about one of the more expensive tape players while I looked at the gun. I checked it out quickly. It was dirty, the slide was sticky, and the barrel was rusted on the inside. You'd probably lose your hand if you tried to fire it. I put it back down on the table and nodded for us to move on.

Besides a handgun, I also needed a shotgun.

That was going to be a lot easier to find. There are more shotguns floating around than any other kind of weapon, and some of them were manufactured so long ago that they don't even have serial numbers on them, but they still work just fine. A shotgun is a very simple weapon. I wouldn't really need to even check it out. Again, I didn't need a high-quality gun. I was going to be sawing off the barrel anyway. I just needed something that would fire when the trigger was pulled, maybe a Rossi, or even something like an old Sears and Roebuck.

We stopped by another van that had a couple of shotguns sitting out. I was looking them over when something inside the van caught my eye. I looked as closely as I could without seeming to be staring. I pulled Willard aside, out of sight of the man seated by his van.

"I found exactly what I want," I said. "The only problem is that you might have some trouble getting him to sell it to you."

"What is it, a machine gun?"

"No, it's a Snake Charmer."

"Ah, of course. A Snake Charmer. Perfect. I should have thought of it myself."

"A Snake Charmer," I explained condescendingly, "is a short-barreled shotgun with a pistol grip. Mostly they are used in the South, where a man walking across the swampy fields will sometimes come across a rattlesnake at his feet and need to deal with it instantly. Thus, I believe, its name."

"Oh."

"The point is, I'm pretty sure the barrel is too short to be legal in California. It's only eighteen inches. That's why it's not outside the van. The guy may be a little leery about selling it."

"If he didn't want to sell it, he wouldn't have brought it here," said Willard reasonably. "I'll talk to him."

He wandered back to the van and got into a conversation with the guy. Fifteen minutes later the man was showing him all kinds of things, talking animatedly. Willard motioned toward the van, the man's voice dropped a little, and he looked out over the passing crowd in a reflex action. Then he shrugged. Then he nodded his head. Willard walked over to the van and looked at something inside, hidden from view. Five minutes later he was walking back toward me carrying a short bundle wrapped in newspaper. I shook my head in admiration.

"Sometimes you amaze me," I said.

"I don't see why. You know me."

That was about as close as Willard comes to bragging, so I knew he was pleased with himself.

The Charmer was a real stroke of luck. The guy would remember Willard, sure enough, but he wouldn't be admitting to anyone that he had sold an illegal gun, especially if he thought it had been used in a crime.

I still needed a small automatic, and I wanted a rifle as well, a good one with a scope. Nothing exotic, a 30.06, probably, just your basic deer rifle. A Winchester or a Remington or maybe a Ruger. A nice common rifle that would be difficult to trace. We searched for about an hour longer, but I didn't see anything else that looked promising.

"How about the Alameda flea market?" Willard suggested. "It's basically the same thing as here, maybe a little smaller, but they have some nice stuff."

Alameda is clear on the other side of San Francisco, but it turned out to be worth the drive, since I found what I was looking for in five minutes, a Remington 700, .243 caliber, in perfect condition, with a 6x Redfield scope. My personal preference in a scope would have been something like a Zeiss or a Leupold, but the Redfield was good enough to do the job. A .243 caliber is a little light, maybe, but it is extremely accurate, and that makes up for a lot. I might have to be trying a very long shot. The man selling it had several other rifles, and a beautiful engraved Browning shotgun, a .20 gauge Invector. He dealt only in quality firearms. "The Remington .243 is the perfect varmint rifle," he told us. I resisted the temptation to say that's exactly what it was going to be used for. People remember comments like that.

There was also a collection of handguns displayed on a long table, including a .25 Beretta auto that would just fit inside my wallet. It could come in very useful. Both guns were expensive, but Willard handled it well, not seeming too eager to buy, but also not spending a long time haggling over price. Either of those things tend to make a customer stick in a man's mind. The guy even threw in a couple of boxes of ammunition.

We stopped on the way back to San Fran-

cisco at a bike store and picked up a motorcycle helmet with a tinted face shield, the kind
you can't see into from outside. I was feeling
pretty good. I had gotten everything I wanted,
which meant I could get back to Salt Lake by
Sunday afternoon. I was exhausted, though,
and crashed almost immediately. I slept until
ten that night, then dragged myself out of bed
and got ready to leave. Willard was in the
kitchen, reading a book entitled *First Aid for
Dogs*. He didn't even own a dog.

"I'm on my way," I said, pouring a cup of
coffee from the pot on the stove.

"Write if you get work."

"Thanks for the help."

He nodded. "Are you sure you want to do
this, Jase?"

"Not really, but I'm going to."

He nodded again. "Be careful."

"Always."

"Good luck."

"I'll see you when it's over," I said, grabbed
my bag, and walked out the door.

NINE

I got back to Salt Lake about noon. I was glad to get home. Stony was sleeping on the couch when I walked in. He looked at me, stretched, and walked out of the room. He was pissed. He didn't like being left alone with nothing interesting to eat.

I was too wired to sleep, so I turned on the TV and watched *The Treasure of the Sierra Madre*, my favorite movie, on cable. When I was a teenager I wanted to be Humphry Bogart. So did every other guy I knew. Kids today have no idea what Bogey meant to us back then. I guess they know who he was, sort of, but they don't know what he meant. "Some actor or something, isn't he?" is the best they can do. As the years roll by, I start identifying less with young people and more with my parents. It's kind of frightening.

On the way out to Marin with Willard, we had been listening to the car radio, and a song by one of the newer punk bands came on the air. It was loud, mostly atonal, the lyrics were indecipherable, and the musicians couldn't play their instruments very well. It was just awful. I turned to Willard and voiced my opinion at length.

"I can't believe the trash being played on the radio these days," I concluded righteously. "Where in God's name do they come up with this crap?"

He turned his head toward me, keeping one eye on the road.

"Does what you're saying ring any kind of a bell?" He smirked. "Think back a few years. Does the term 'rock music' sound familiar?"

"That's entirely different."

"Oh?"

"No, it is."

"How so, Jase?"

"It's obvious. Back then the music was new, full of energy. It had something to say. It had . . . you know, soul."

"And nobody over thirty could stand it."

"Yeah, but they were listening to Lawrence Welk. They were wrong and we were right, simple as that. You're right about one thing, nothing has changed. We're still right. The only difference is that now it's the kids who don't know their ass from a hole in the ground, musically speaking."

Willard didn't say anything more, but the smirk remained on his face. I have a sneaking suspicion that it isn't different at all, but I'll never admit it. I watched *Sierra Madre* until the gold dust blew off into the wind, and then I took a nap.

It was dark when Stony finally woke me up by jumping on my head to let me know dinner was overdue. He knew better, since I usually threw him against the wall if he woke me up, but I guess he felt I deserved some sort of payback for being away. I gave him something to eat, put a hammer and large screwdriver in a backpack, threw in a roll of electrical tape, picked up the motorcycle helmet I had brought back, and went out to do a night's work.

Eleven to midnight is a good time to be out on the streets if you're up to no good. It's late enough that there aren't a lot of people on the streets to see what you are doing, but still early enough so the patrol cops aren't looking that carefully yet at those who are.

I parked my car at the all-night Safeway on Second South, in the back of the lot, and started walking through the neighborhood, strolling along, just another fellow out for the night air. A lot of students from the U of U live up in that area, which is why I picked it. College students may be a lot different these days, but there is one thing that hasn't changed. An awful lot of them own motorcycles. I found just the bike I wanted on a side street off 13th East, a 360 Honda with a Windjammer fairing on it, maybe eight or nine years old. It was parked in front of a duplex. The lights were still on in the right-side apartment, but I couldn't see anybody when I looked through the window of the front room. If I was lucky, they were in the back and wouldn't be glancing out the window at just the wrong moment. I didn't like having to take that chance, but there isn't any way to be 100 percent safe all the time. All you can do is cut down the odds as much as possible.

I opened my backpack as I walked up toward the bike, and when I got alongside, pulled out the hammer and screwdriver, bending over the front forks. The tip of the screwdriver went in the key slot next to the forks. I hit the handle a sharp blow with the hammer, driving the screwdriver into the lock cylinder, then gave the screwdriver a sharp twist. The lock snapped as I turned the handle, and the forks were free. I pulled out the screwdriver, which stuck fast for an instant, worrying me momentarily. As soon as the lock was free, I straightened up and walked on down the street. The noise the hammer made when it struck the end of the screwdriver wasn't loud, but the street was quiet and it might have been just enough to make someone wonder and look out.

I made a quick loop around the block. There was no sign anyone had noticed anything. I took the helmet out of my pack and slipped it over my head. If anyone did see me now they wouldn't think twice about it, except, of course, the owner of the bike. Anyone who sees someone messing around with a bike at midnight might well take a second look to see what's going on. But if you're wearing a motorcycle helmet, they naturally assume you belong with the bike. It also helps that no one is going to be able to describe you later on.

I took hold of the three wires that led into the ignition between the handlebars and gave them a hard yank. They came out with no trouble at all. I stripped the ends bare with my pocketknife, turned on the gas shut-off valve, and wrapped two of the wires together with the electrical tape. I touched them with the third wire, the one that led out of the starter motor, and the engine turned over as sweet as you please. So far the whole thing had taken about a minute and a half. Now I could only hope that the owner kept his bike tuned up properly. It would not be a good idea to spend five minutes there in front of the owner's house trying to get a cranky bike to start.

Thankfully, I found that it was well maintained. Five seconds later I was riding down the street on my new bike.

I was exultant, far more than I would be just by accomplishing a task. It was like the good old days. I understood all over again just how it is so difficult to rehabilitate anyone, especially a burglar or thief. You can teach them skills, find them jobs, counsel them all you want, but it doesn't change one basic fact: Walking up and stealing a motorcycle is a rush. Getting away with it provides a feeling of great satisfaction. Working in a grocery store, even at good wages, just doesn't provide the same thrill. Once you get started, it's not easy to stop. It's a lot like drugs. Of course, you can always become a cop.

I cruised along Foothill Drive, carefully observing the speed limit, when a black-and-white came up on my tail. There was no way the bike could have been reported stolen yet, so I just kept on driving the same speed, trying to look innocent and harmless. The patrol car flipped on his overheads. Apparently he had decided to check me out, for whatever reason. I held up my right hand to signal, and pulled off to the side of the road. The patrolman got out of the car slowly, so the stolen bike wasn't the problem. I watched him come up in the rearview mirror. It was Dennis Patchco, a guy who'd been on the department for five years or so. He was known as a hard charger, just the type that would stop a motorcycle on a whim, just to see if he could find something wrong. I waited until he was about four steps away and gunned it. I could hear him curse as he sprinted back toward his car. I cut down the first side street I saw. With any luck I could lose him before he ever had a chance to get back up to me.

I didn't get the luck. Just as I turned, another set of overheads came up fast. A backup car had arrived, swooping in just as I took off, and the chase was on.

I'd been in many a chase before, but it was a lot more fun from the other side. From my viewpoint, it was the worst time of day for a chase. As long as there is traffic on the road, a motorcycle has an immense advantage, but when the streets are clear, that edge evaporates. I twisted through the residential streets with a black-and-white on my tail, tires squealing. A third car joined in, blocking the end of the street I had turned onto. I ran up the sidewalk and over a lawn to get past him.

He pointed his gun at me as I passed, screaming his head off, but I knew he wouldn't shoot. As far as he knew, I was just a kid on a bike running from the cops. As I flew past, I could hear the siren of still another car coming up from the left.

I came out the side streets onto 17th South, one of the pursuing cars no more than twenty feet behind me now. I was trying to make it to the small park east of 17th South. There is a narrow street that dead-ends at one end of the park. A long flight of narrow stone steps gives access to pedestrians, but that's the only way in from that side. When I reached the dead end by the steps, instead of stopping, I pointed the bike up the stairs and accelerated. The bike twisted when I hit the first step and I almost lost it right there, but I just managed to keep it under control. The black-and-white behind me didn't fare quite so well. He hit the bottom of the stairway, stomped on his brakes, bounced up on two wheels, and almost flipped over. I made it to the top of the stairs, every bounce jarring my teeth, and sped across the grass meadow there toward the opposite side of the park. I almost ran over a couple who were lying on the grass, making out in the dark. I'll bet the guy never got her to go up there with him again.

As soon as I hit the street on the other side of the park, I turned off my headlight and made it over to 21st South, one of the main thoroughfares. I pulled in behind a small service station and parked the bike between the back of the station and a tire rack full of old retreads. For the next hour I waited. About half an hour after I had pulled in, a patrol car swung by and flashed his spot toward the back, but didn't stop. I wanted another hour. Finally I eased out and drove cautiously home. I didn't see another car the whole way. It was two A.M. when I finally slipped into my garage.

It took about half an hour to change the license plate to my satisfaction, using scissors and the roll of electrical tape. The bike had one of the old-style plates, with black lettering on a white background, and some judicious work with the tape turned a one into a seven and a three into an eight. It wouldn't stand close inspection, but at ten feet, the average distance of a patrol car sitting behind another vehicle, it was indistinguishable from a valid plate. I was pretty safe unless someone decided to stop me again, and that rarely happens in daytime.

My car was still parked down at the Safeway lot, but leaving it there overnight was no problem. I could take a cab down to the U tomorrow morning, walk over to the Safeway, and get it then. What I needed now was some more sleep. I tried, but I didn't get much.

Monday was a holiday, the twenty-fourth of July. In Utah the twenty-fourth is Pioneer Day, sort of a cross between the Fourth of July and New Year's Eve. It celebrates the arrival of the Mormons into the Salt Lake Valley, back in 1847, and is the most important holiday in the state. For the first five years I was on the department, I had to work the annual parade, and I got to hate Pioneer Day with a passion.

The Courts Building was closed, but the schedule of cases for the next day was posted on the door of the main entrance. I found the listing for Edward Wrones. The hearing on his parole violation was scheduled for room C-205, Judge Conklin's courtroom, 9:00 A.M. Tuesday morning. Wrones should be coming in from the prison about eight.

There wasn't anything I could do now but wait, so I drove downtown to watch the floats go by. It was the first time I had actually seen the entire parade. Talk about peculiar. Every other float seemed to be promoting the virtues of chastity or milk. Imagine the parade at the Rose Bowl sponsored by an extremely conservative religious organization, and you get some idea of what it's like.

When I left the parade I parked my car in the Albertson's supermarket parking lot, about six blocks from the main station. I walked back to the downtown area, which took me about twenty minutes, and took a cab back home again. I spent some time that evening polishing up my new motorcycle, going over every surface on the bike with an oily rag, then a dry one. I did the same thing with my helmet, and then the Snake Charmer, which I loaded. The Charmer is a simple breakdown single-barrel gun. It holds only one round, but one round was all I was going to need.

By the time I was through, there wasn't a single fingerprint anywhere on the bike or the gun or the helmet. An old red windbreaker came out of the basement where it had been lying in a corner for God knows how long. It was torn and dirty, and I hadn't worn it for a couple of years, but I'm one of those people who never seems to throw anything out. My whole basement, in fact, looks like a rummage sale with nothing worth buying.

From now on, I wouldn't even go near any of the items I was going to be using until I was ready to move. It's easier than you think to touch something without realizing it. After all my work and planning, it would be ironic if something as obvious as a fingerprint were to trip me up.

It would take me about twenty-five minutes to drive from my house to the freeway off-ramp, so I set my alarm for six-thirty. I wanted to give myself plenty of time to get ready. I had trouble getting to sleep again that night, which wasn't surprising, but I finally dropped off about two. The sound of the garbage truck outside picking up trash woke me, and I groaned. I had forgotten to take out the garbage the night before. One second later I remembered, and jumped out of bed in a panic. The garbage truck usually came by about seven-thirty. My alarm hadn't gone off. I looked at my clock. It was 7:28. I stifled my feeling of despair. I still had time to make it if I was lucky. I wasn't going to get my morning cup of coffee, though, and I wasn't going to have the luxury of being able to think things over one last time.

I threw on my clothes, opened my dresser drawer, and pulled out a pair of rubber surgeon's gloves. I ripped open the sterile pack and carefully put them on. I still had about four pairs, which I had picked up from the hospital emergency room back when I was working patrol. All patrol cops, at least those who have been on the job for a while, carry them. They are extremely useful for picking up dead bodies, searching sick derelicts, and other unpleasant tasks that make up a great deal of a patrolman's life. You can do anything with them on that you can do with your bare hands, and of course, they don't leave any prints. We always tried to cadge a few extra pairs when we got a hospital call. The nurses were pretty good about handing them out.

I slipped the windbreaker over my shirt, picked up the Snake Charmer, pulled the helmet over my head, and flipped the face shield down. I ran into the garage, started up the bike, and stuck the Charmer in the side pocket of the fairing. It poked out just a little, but there were some rags in the pocket partially covering it, and you couldn't tell what it was just by looking at it. I was on the road exactly seven minute after the garbage truck woke me up.

I was in a real fix. If I drove too fast, I might get stopped. That would be the end of my plans. If I kept to the speed limit, I would get there just around eight, and that might be too late. I took the chance and pushed it. I was lucky; there wasn't a cop in sight all the way. I got to the off-ramp at ten minutes before eight and pulled over to the side of Fourth West, where I could see the cars coming off the ramp. I might have missed them already if they were particularly early this morning, but the odds were in my favor that they hadn't been. I sat there watching the cars come down the ramp, almost beside myself with fear that I had blown it. At the same time, in the back of my mind, I was almost hoping that I had. Now that I was right up against it, I didn't like it. I didn't like it at all. I realized I was whistling a monotone again.

About eight o'clock I saw the prison car, bringing in Fat Eddie for his parole violation hearing. It was a plain white car with only a gray decal on the side to identify it, but I knew it immediately. I had seen those cars often enough before. It was already starting to be a warm day, and both front windows were rolled down. The prison budget didn't allow for air conditioning in the cars, although the guards had complained about it for years. They claimed it created a security risk, and they were right. They ought to be thanking me, though. I was going to get their air conditioning for them.

Fat Eddie was sitting in the front passenger seat next to the driver, presumably handcuffed. The other guard was in the back seat, sitting directly behind him. It was good transport procedure. You never want your prisoner behind you, unless you have a cage car with a secure shield, and the prison didn't use cage cars unless the inmate was actively violet. If you are the second guard in the car, you want to be behind your man where you can watch him, not the other way around.

As soon as I saw the car, an adrenaline rush hit me like a wall. I put the bike in motion, and as I shifted the gear lever I realized that my foot was shaking. Swinging into the flow of traffic, I followed the prison car, keeping about three cars back. We swept through the light at Third West, then at Second West, and again at West Temple. This was something I hadn't considered. What if they made all the lights and didn't have to stop until reaching the jail? I had never been able to manage that, but it was possible. At morning rush hour, though, there was just too much traffic to keep up the pace and make all the lights. The signal at Main Street turned red, and the line of traffic finally came to a halt.

It was now or never. I pulled slowly past the stopped cars between me and the prison car and came up on the passenger side right beside Fat Eddie. He was staring straight ahead, and didn't even notice me. The guard in the back seat did and looked at me curiously. Without thinking about it, and in one motion, I grabbed the pistol grip, pulled the Charmer out of the fairing pocket, leaned slightly toward the car, put the barrel in Fat Eddie's face, and pulled the trigger. His head jerked violently back, and his face exploded. The sound of the gun going off was surprisingly loud, even with the helmet on. I could see everything in minute detail, a slow-motion display of blood and tissue splattering on the roof of the car, on the driver, and on the guard in the backseat. The guard's face was frozen in shock, but his hand was frantically reaching under his jacket, trying to get his gun free. The driver was motionless, staring at me with his mouth open. The tableau seemed to go on forever.

I dropped the Charmer in the street and gunned the bike. The driver, to give him credit, reacted almost instantly, swerving around the car in front of him, trying to come after me. In the first few seconds I was afraid of one of them taking a shot at me, although it would have been an incredibly stupid thing to do. The chances of hitting a moving target while shooting from a moving vehicle yourself, especially with a handgun, are not even worth thinking about. The chances of a shot instead hitting a pedestrian on a crowded street are very good. Any police officer with training knows this, but in the heat of the moment, sometimes people forget.

After those first seconds went by, I knew I was safe. There were no shots fired from the prison car. The driver of the car tried his best to catch up with me, but there is no way a car can follow a motorcycle in downtown rush-hour traffic.

I weaved in and out of the traffic lanes, squeezed past the cars waiting at the light on Fifth South, and ducked around the block. The prison car was stuck behind a delivery van, totally impotent. They didn't even have a radio with the city frequency on it. By the time they contacted the statewide frequency dispatcher and got the information relayed to the city cops in the area, it was too late.

I drove the bike three blocks down West Temple until I reached the Crossroads Mall parking terrace, a seven-story complex that services the downtown area's biggest mall. I rode into the entrance, took a ticket from the machine, and rode up to the fourth level. There weren't a lot of cars around that early, since a lot of the stores in the mall don't open until nine, and there was no one nearby that I could see. I parked the bike behind a support pillar, where I was momentarily out of view, and jerked the wires to the ignition apart, shutting down the engine. I took off the helmet and laid it on the seat, pulled off my windbreaker, and stripped off my gloves. Then I walked unhurriedly into the mall, took the escalator to the ground floor, and walked out the Main Street exit on the other side. As I left the mall, I could hear sirens heading toward Sixth South. I just kept walking. Twenty minutes later, I was in my car at the supermarket and twenty-five minutes after that I was pulling into my driveway at home. Stony was sitting on the front stoop, and meowed a greeting as I walked up to the door. I reached down and pulled his tail absently.

"If you only knew how simple your life is," I told him, and went inside.

TEN

A half hour after I got home, I started shaking. I had been so intent on what I was doing that I hadn't thought of anything else. Now the reaction was starting to set in. My mouth was dry, and I kept trying to swallow, but my throat didn't seem to be working right.

I don't know how I expected to feel—I didn't feel bad or sorry or anything like that, but I didn't feel very good about it either. I guess what I mostly felt was drained.

I turned on the TV. There was a movie on TBS, but I don't remember what it was. At eleven a baseball game came on, Atlanta versus the Mets, and Dwight Gooden was pitching. It's funny how you can watch something and not really watch it. I was aware of every play. If you had asked me, I could have told you what happened to the last three batters, but at the same time, I wasn't really watching at all. There was an instant replay machine in my head, and the tape kept running over and over.

I wondered how long it would take before someone downtown got the idea that I might be involved with the shooting, and how long after that it would be before they sent someone over to talk with me. I figured it wouldn't be until tomorrow morning at the earliest. It would take them a while to convince themselves that it was possible, and then a little longer to realize that they had no choice but to check me out.

Then again, Dave Warren at least was going to pick up on it right away. Even if no one else figured it, he would. The question was, would he bring it up to Volter? Knowing Dave, I voted yes. It might be hard for him, but at heart he was a cop first. He wouldn't let our friendship stand in the way of what he would see as his responsibility to his job. When he did say something about his suspicions, Volter might well decide to send someone over right away. The idea of getting to a suspect fast is standard interrogation technique. Anyone who commits a violent crime is shaken, sometimes even bad enough to cop to it if you get to them right away. Once they get a night's sleep under their belt, it's a whole different ball game.

But Volter had an extra problem—who was going to talk to me? Dave was the natural choice, since he was far and away the best investigator in homicide, and the sergeant recognized that. But Dave and I had been pretty close over the years, and Volter was aware of that, too. He didn't know Dave as well as I did, and might well wonder if Dave would press me as hard as he really should. He couldn't be sure just how complete Dave's investigation would be. God knew how Dave really felt about the situation. Given all that, I didn't see how Volter could send him over.

Of course, he couldn't send someone like Becker either. Becker was a smart cop, but I despised Becker, as Volter well knew. I wouldn't tell Becker shit was brown. As I saw it, Volter's only real option was to show up himself, and to bring one of the nonentities with him as a backup—someone like Choames or Bodley, guys who didn't have an enemy in the world, guys I would feel neutral about, and vice versa. Unfortunately, neither Choames nor Bodley had enough investigative ability to discover a murder in a phone booth. Still, you can't have everything. All in all, coming in person and bringing one of them along with him would be the best thing to do.

After a couple of hours I got up and made myself a ham sandwich, but I couldn't eat it. It tasted like plasterboard mixed with chalk dust. I had to chew the first bite about thirty times before I could swallow, and I didn't try a second one.

At noon I switched over the channel to the local news. The downtown shooting was the lead story. They had pictures of the paramedics working on Fat Eddie, and the ambulance rushing him to the hospital. I had a moment's anxiety, although I knew that there absolutely was no chance he could have survived the blast. A .410 is not a very large bore shotgun, but when it goes off in your face, there's not a whole lot left to work with. Still, I didn't relax completely until the newscaster mentioned that the victim had been pronounced D.O.A. at the hospital. Police, he continued, had no suspects as yet, but were following several leads. I'll just bet they are, I thought.

The news shifted on to other stories, and with perfect timing a plain white Chevy Malibu pulled up in front of the house. Two men got out, Volter and Fletcher Choames, and I had a momentary surge of satisfaction at having guessed it right. I waited for the doorbell to ring before I opened the door. I didn't want them to think I was expecting them. They would understand how it was soon enough without any help from me.

Mike Volter seemed ill at ease when he came in. I realized I didn't know him all that well, although I had worked with him for years. He wasn't a bad cop; he just had no imagination. Anything out of the ordinary made him uncomfortable, and questioning a fellow cop about a homicide is not exactly your everyday routine. I offered him a chair, and he sat down heavily. Choames, as usual, was totally oblivious, staring around the room. Probably he was trying to assess the value of the house and contents. Choames sold Amway products in his free time.

Mike noticed that the news was still on, and it gave him an opening. He moved his big frame uneasily in the chair and cleared his throat.

"Did you see the story?" he asked.

I nodded.

"Let me tell you, Jase, it was a bad scene. The news media were all over the place. The chief himself came down and looked things over. He told me that if I didn't solve this one pretty damn quick, there was going to be another sergeant running homicide."

"I can just hear him," I said, commiserating.

"Yeah, this is not a good situation," he repeated.

I nodded again. "I can see that."

Mike was waiting for me to give him some kind of opening to broach the subject, but I wasn't giving him any help. I really felt kind of sorry for him. There was a silence for about ten seconds before he realized I wasn't going to offer any more in the way of comment. He finally gathered himself and plunged in.

"Jason," he started, "you're not stupid. You know why we're here. Everyone on the department knows what happened with that girl and understands how you must have felt about this guy. Hell, I understand myself; if anything happened to my wife, I'd feel the same way. If it were up to me, I'd just write the bastard off as one less maggot for society to worry about."

That was a joke. I might not know Mike all that well, but I did know him better than that. He'd do a case on his own grandmother if he thought he could make it stick. Still, it was a good line. He plowed ahead, ignoring the expression on my face.

"It isn't up to me, though," he continued. "I've got to follow every line of investigation, no matter where it leads, no matter how I might personally feel about it. So I'm afraid there are some questions I've got to ask."

"No problem, Mike," I said. Relief was evident on his face. "Are you going to read me Miranda?"

I smiled as I spoke, just to show there were no hard feelings. He didn't smile back. A worried look appeared.

"I guess maybe I'd better," he said heavily, and took out his wallet, extracting an old and battered Miranda card which he held in front of him. I couldn't believe that he was still reading Miranda off the card instead of having it memorized. He had been reading people their rights for some fifteen years, for God's sake. A lot of cops are like that, though. They're afraid some lawyer will make a big deal out of it in court if it isn't read word for word every time off the card.

"Jason, you have the right to remain silent. Anything you say can and will be used against you in a court of law. You have the right to consult with an attorney before answering any questions, and to have an attorney present with you during any questioning. If you cannot afford an attorney, one will be appointed for you by the court at no cost to yourself. If at any time during questioning, you wish to stop answering questions, you are free to do so, and no more questions will be asked." He put the card back in his wallet.

"Do you understand each of these rights as I have explained them to you?"

"Yes, I do."

"Keeping these rights in mind, are you now

willing to answer some questions about the death of Edward Wrones?''

This was the big moment. Up to now, I don't think he really believed I had anything to do with the shooting. He knew me; I was a cop. Cops don't do things like that, at least not in his world. Sure, there was always a chance, and it had to be checked out, but he was still more embarrassed by the situation than anything else. He expected I would tell him where I had been that morning, then one of the detectives would check it out and confirm the alibi, and then he could apologize, cross me off the list, and start working on finding the real killer. I shook my head slowly.

"No, Mike," I said deliberately. "I don't think I want to talk to you."

I had never thought of Mike Volter as having a particularly expressive face, but the range of emotions evident on it now was just amazing. First, there was a kind of blank expression while he tried to assimilate what I had just said. Next came the dawning awareness that perhaps it was true, that maybe I really had shot Fat Eddie, an awareness that hardened into instant conviction. Then the doubt crept back in. I could almost see his thought process working, like a little balloon over his head. It is perfectly normal for anyone connected to law enforcement, innocent or guilty, to want to keep silent until they have had time to think a situation over. It didn't necessarily mean I had anything to hide. But it sure looked and sounded bad. Belief in my guilt returned to his features. Finally there was the realization of just what doing an investigation on me was going to entail, not to mention what would happen if the press found out that I was being considered as a suspect. I had definitely ruined his day.

Choames was looking at me, his mouth hanging wide open. He looked like a confused trout. Even he was beginning to get the idea that there was a very large can of worms being opened before his very eyes.

We all sat there. No one said a word. The sound of the neighborhood kids shouting obscenities on the street came drifting through the window. Finally Mike cleared his throat again.

"You realize what this is going to look like," he said tightly.

"I can't help that."

He sat there for a few more moments and then rose to his feet and walked to the door. Choames trailed silently behind him. I stood in the doorway and watched as he and Choames got into their car and drove away. They didn't look back.

If I were Mike Volter, I would be a worried man about now. Most homicides are not planned. Usually they're a result of overpowering passion or rage, or a situation gone bad, out of control. As a result, there are leads. Those rare murders that are a result of careful planning have a motive, and with a little digging, that motive can be uncovered. When you find the motive, nine times out of ten you also find a suspect. That suspect will go to great lengths to provide himself with a complicated alibi and rational explanation for his actions on the day of the murder. First and foremost in his mind is the desire to avoid suspicion, and to do that, he must at least appear to be cooperating with the detectives. He has to talk to them, show them around, and in every way possible indicate he has nothing to hide. And this is precisely what provides the opening.

My reaction presented a different problem, a difficult one. I didn't care whether he suspected me or not. I didn't care if he knew I did it or not. All I cared about was not getting caught and sent to jail. The only thing that concerned me was what they could prove, not what they believed. In a way, I was taking advantage of the system, the same way Jennifer's killers had done. I had no intention of providing an opening by talking to Volter or anyone else.

When someone stonewalls, the only way to prove anything is through physical evidence. They had the shotgun. Pretty soon they would have the motorcycle, although the windbreaker and helmet would probably be ripped off before anyone noticed the bike. But none of those things would do them a whole lot of good unless they could connect them up with me, and I really didn't think they could.

What I had to do now was to keep one step ahead of them. Dave would be pretty sure I would go after Holzer next, but I thought it would take some doing on his part to convince the others on the squad. People just don't go on one-man vendettas, at least not as a rule.

They would need some time to adjust to the idea, time I could put to good use. Keep moving, keep hitting them, that was the idea, and it was time to get on it again.

ELEVEN

As I drove to a phone booth, I kept looking in the rearview mirror to see if I was being followed. There was no way Volter would have gotten anything going yet, or even begun to decide what to do about me, but I couldn't help it.

I called Allred's office number and the same cheery receptionist answered. She informed me Allred wasn't expected to be in the office this afternoon. I imagine that Fat Eddie's death and its implications had shaken him a little.

"I need to talk with him real bad," I said. "It's about the murder of one of his clients, Edward Wrones. I have some information about it that he ought to know. Tell him I'm the same guy who called a couple of week ago

162

about the pickup truck. I'll call back at five-thirty.

I hung up without waiting for a reply. I knew she would get the message to him; she'd be afraid not to. He would be there at five-thirty, too. There was no way he could ignore that call.

At exactly five-thirty I called back, I didn't care if he recognized my voice or not. For my purposes, it didn't really matter. This time there was no cheerful secretary on the line. He answered it himself.

"Allred speaking."

"Julian Allred? Julian P. Allred? Juley?"

"Who is this?"

"Not important. What's important is what I've got to say."

"Then say it. I don't have time to play games."

"Well, I'll tell you. It's about a little ride down State Street that you took with Jack Holzer and that fat slob that got wasted today. I hear that was one pretty girl that got snuffed. And that girl up in City Creek. Now that was a big mistake." I changed to a confidential tone.

"You poor fucker, don't you know who that girl was? Her boyfriend was a cop. He's the one who did Fat Eddie this morning. What do you think would happen if he got wind of you?"

Allred must have been a little jarred, but his composure didn't slip for an instant. He wasn't a lawyer for nothing.

"If you have any information about a killing," he said coldly, "I suggest you contact the police department."

"You know, I thought of that. I did. I might even just do that. But I don't really want to tell anyone about anything. I'd much rather take a vacation, and to do that, I'm going to need about fifty thousand dollars."

Allred laughed. "Good luck."

"I don't need luck. I've got you. Let me put it to you this way. Either I get some money, or I call the cops. Not only that, but I call one particular cop. He might be interested in knowing who was with fat boy that night. How long do you think you would last? A week? Two? He did a pretty slick job on your fat friend, didn't he?"

Allred took all this in without comment, deciding how to handle it. He finally decided to play dumb.

"Whoever you are, you've got hold of some bad information. I don't have the slightest idea what you're talking about."

"Sure, pal. However you want to play it. Fifty thousand dollars, tomorrow morning at nine. The banks open at eight. I'll meet you in the parking lot by the Snowpine Lodge at Alta. Leave that psycho Holzer out of it. If you're not there alone with the money, I'll be making some phone calls."

I hung up the phone without giving him a chance to say anything else. I thought it had gone pretty well. The first thing he would do would be to call Holzer and talk it over. My name would come up. If Allred hadn't heard yet I was a prime suspect in the Fat Eddie case, he soon would. He had good sources. They would come up with two possibilities. Either I was a blackmailer who had actually seen them, or, far more likely, I was Jason Coulter. Allred might buy the blackmail idea. That's the kind of lawyer mind he had. Holzer was street smart, though. He would smell a rat, a setup. That's the way he thought. That's the kind of thing he would do in my position. But either way, blackmailer or cop, they couldn't afford to ignore me. They would show up at the Snowpine Lodge, but they wouldn't be bringing any money. They would be there to kill me and solve the problem once and for all.

I went home and locked the Remington in the trunk of my car. A couple of ham sandwiches and a quart of grape juice in a plastic water bottle went into my backpack. I drove out west of the airport to the desert and spent an hour sighting in the rifle. It was pretty good, throwing just a little to the right, and a minor scope adjustment fixed that. As soon as it started to get dark, I grabbed my Walther, just in case, and took off for Big Cottonwood Canyon. I also took along a warm jacket and a pair of leather gloves. It gets cold up in the canyons at night, even in summer. I wasn't so worried about prints this time. I was planning to dump the rifle where no one would ever find it, or at least not for a good many years. Big and Little Cottonwood canyons are both riddled with open mine shafts, relics from the turn of the century when Alta was a boomtown, boasting some of the richest silver and lead mines in the West. Many of those shafts were hundreds of feet deep and so unsafe that no one ever went down in them. Anything thrown down those shafts would stay there.

I got to the Silverfork branch of Big Cottonwood just after dusk and pulled my car off the road where it was hidden by a stand of elderberry bushes. I started up the fork, with the rifle slung over my back. It was dark enough now so that no one would see me. I didn't want the sheriff's department investigating a report of a man seen carrying a rifle. The whole area was becoming populated enough so that a man carrying a rifle, especially out of hunting season, got noticed.

I'd been hiking the trails in the canyons for ten years, and I didn't have any trouble finding my way, even in the dark. It took me a couple of hours to cross over the ridge connecting Big to Little Cottonwood, where the Snowpine is located. There wasn't any moon, but I could see enough by starlight to make my way.

About midnight I reached the spot I had been aiming for. Right across the road from the parking lot by the Snowpine is a flat rock ledge, about two hundred yards up the side of the mountain. If you lie down flat there, you can't be seen from the lot down below. It was the perfect vantage point for a sniper, and even a poor shot would find it difficult to miss a target in the parking lot.

That wasn't where I headed, though. I was headed farther up the mountainside, to a small thicket of trees and bushes about two hundred yards past the rock ledge. Once inside the trees, I was totally hidden. I could no longer see the parking lot very well, and it was a little too far away for a confident shot, but I had a perfect view of the rock ledge.

This is the way I read it: Holzer would figure that I was setting up Allred for a hit. A quick meet in the parking lot, and it would be all over. So what Holzer would do would be to get there early and set up in a place where he could ambush me from above. The perfect place for doing that, maybe the only good place, was the rock ledge. It would leap out as the logical place to hide with a rifle. In the unlikely event it turned out to be just a black-mailer after all, there was no reason to change the scenario. One shot would do the trick. Allred would jump in his car, Holzer would scoot over the other side of the ridge and be picked up in Big Cottonwood. It was a perfectly sound plan. The only flaw in it was that when Holzer lay down on the rock ledge to wait for me to show up below, I wouldn't be there. I'd be above him with a perfect shot. I wouldn't have a shot at Allred, but I couldn't have everything. I could deal with him later. Holzer was the target now.

I settled in for the night. It was actually pretty comfortable, and I sat there, back propped up against a tree, smoking a cigarette and listening to the night noises. Night in the mountains isn't like night outdoors most places. No crickets chirping, no small animals rustling in the underbrush—none of the sounds usually associated with woods at night. Only the sound of the wind blowing through the aspens, and the occasional far-off crashing of deer breaking through a thicket. I sat back against a tree, cradling my rifle and feeling ludicrously at peace.

I must have dropped off for a while, for the next thing I noticed was the sky just beginning to get light. I ate a sandwich, drank some juice, and lit another cigarette. The birds were just beginning to stir, but everywhere else it was that early morning quiet. Far off, I heard the sound of a car engine coming up the canyon road. As it grew closer, I looked out to see what I could, although there was barely enough light yet to make out the road.

The car, a Toyota, I thought, pulled up in the parking lot by the Snowpine. Allred drove a BMW, but that didn't mean anything. I hadn't expected him to be using his own car. It had to be Allred and Holzer. I looked through the scope, but it was still too dark to distinguish faces. They were both wearing baseball caps. They got out, stretched, and leaned against the car hood. They stood there for a while, talking in low tones, the sound perfectly audible in the early morning air, although I couldn't make out the words. A couple of times they laughed briefly.

As soon as it was a little lighter, one of the men started looking around. At length, he pointed up at the rock ledge above the parking lot, reached into the car, and pulled out a rifle. Then he said something else to the other man and started up the hillside toward the ledge. The bill of the cap covered his face, but it was Holzer. Allred was going to be the bait.

It took him only ten minutes to reach the ledge, and he lay down flat, looking over the edge. He waved at the man down below. I put the scope on the parking lot again, and when the man looked up there was enough light to recognize Allred's face under the brim. Allred waved back at him and then drove off down the canyon road. Apparently they were guessing I would get there early. If Allred was already in the parking lot when I arrived, I might get spooked and start looking around. But if I thought I had gotten there first, and could see Allred drive up alone, I might be less on guard. And if I got there early and stepped out of my car to look around, Holzer would take care of things right then and there.

It was just about five, and the light was now good enough. There was no point in waiting any longer. I eased the Remington through the trees and rested the stock on a crook made by the branches of two trees jammed up against each other. I didn't let the barrel touch the tree. That can throw off your shot. Holzer was lying flat, looking down over the canyon. He didn't know I was within ten miles. I looked through the scope and lined up the cross hairs on the middle of his back. He was wearing a dark short-sleeved shirt. The back of it was soaked through with sweat, even in the chill morning air. He must have been feeling as nervous as I was. His arms were tan and muscular, surprisingly so for a man of his build. I could see his hand on his rifle, caressing it, waiting impatiently for me to arrive. I could barely make out the outline of a tattoo on the hand, a dragon with its tail curling up over his wrist.

I took a deep breath and let it halfway out. The scope steadied. Sight picture, breathing, smooth trigger pull. Those are the simple secrets of accuracy. My finger tightened slowly on the trigger. Then it hit me. I had seen Holzer only once before, in court, but I had looked at him closely. I was willing to swear that he didn't have a tattoo on either hand then. It hardly seemed likely that he would have acquired one in the last two weeks. I eased off the trigger and looked intently through the scope, trying to get a glimpse of his face, but all I could see was the back of his head. The hair was darker than I remembered, and longer. I pulled the rifle back slowly and crouched in the cover of the bushes. What the hell was going on? If that wasn't Holzer, who was it? And if that wasn't Holzer down there, were the hell was he?

As soon as that thought crossed my mind, I automatically pressed myself into the ground, although I knew I couldn't be seen through the trees. The question of where Holzer might be hiding suddenly took on a whole new significance. He might solicit some help, but he wasn't the type to stay at home. He was somewhere close, that was for sure. In fact, I realized belatedly, he was probably somewhere above me on the mountainside. I wasn't in control of this situation, the way I had imagined. Holzer was.

It was becoming clear that I had underestimated Holzer, and underestimated him badly. I had set up a simple trap, but he had looked it over and taken it a step further. He hadn't bought the blackmail scheme at all. I hadn't expected him to, but he hadn't bought the ambush idea either. He knew I was going to be at the Snowpine, and he must have figured I would try something tricky. If he had come up yesterday and looked over the terrain, he would have spotted the rock ledge at once. That was the problem. It was just too perfect a location. Holzer wasn't stupid. I had done a very efficient job on Fat Eddie. He must have understood I would be expecting him to scout the area early and see the ledge. And if I was expecting that, I wouldn't show up down in the parking lot, or up on the ledge either. I would take pains to be somewhere higher, waiting for him to stretch out on that rock shelf, ambushing the ambusher.

The next step was obvious. Set me up in turn. All that was needed was a mention to one of his biker pals. Allred was going to meet someone in the parking lot, someone who needed to be take care of. No fuss, no danger. His friend with the rifle expected an easy shot. It didn't bother Holzer at all that his pal would be killed, as long as I could be taken care of as well. Maybe the guy had pissed him off sometime in the past, and he was killing two birds with one stone, so to speak.

The minute I fired, my position would be revealed. When I came out of cover, I could be picked off with ease. Holzer had done the same thing I had done, only a little later. He had hiked up over the ridge and was waiting now, somewhere up above me.

Of course, he could have just taken up his position without all that other stuff, but the beauty of his plan was that if I was foolish enough to actually show up in the parking lot or try to make it up to the ledge, I was dead anyway. His buddy would cut me down. He had it covered either way. If it hadn't been for that tattoo on the hand where there shouldn't have been one, it would have worked.

I should have seen all this beforehand, but I hadn't thought it through. I had assumed my plan would work, mostly because I wanted it to. Now I sat in the bushes, helpless. There was nothing I could do except wait it out. Holzer couldn't be absolutely positive I was really in the canyon. I might have just been trying to stir them up a little. If I waited until night again, I could hike back over the ridge to my car and be safe. Holzer wouldn't wait that long, and even if he did, he couldn't hit anything in the dark. He would disappear, and wait for another day.

At nine o'clock Allred drove up into the lot again. He studiously avoided looking up at the ledge, and the man who was up there flattened himself even farther into the rock face. By nine-thirty they were both growing tense, and at ten Allred finally looked up to the ledge and waved the man down. There was still no sign of Holzer. The man on the ledge clambered back down, stopping beside the car for a moment to talk to Allred. Then he put the rifle back in the car and they left.

After about an hour I was beginning to think that I had been wrong. Maybe I had read too much into the situation. Maybe Holzer had decided to let someone else handle things, for whatever reason. Still, I couldn't take the chance. I just sat there in the cover of the trees and waited. About two, I ate my other sandwich and drank a little of the juice. I had squirmed around so that I could see out of the trees if I looked up toward the ridge and kept an eye on the area above me, but there was nothing to see. It was a long day.

By dusk I had pretty well decided I had been mistaken, when I saw a figure up on the ridge line, barely visible. I looked through the scope and could see that whoever it was, he was carrying a rifle, and he was headed over the ridge into Big Cottonwood. I had missed him when he came out of cover. As I watched, the figure crested the top and disappeared from view. I had been right, but there was no satisfaction in it. I had alerted both Allred and Holzer and had gotten nothing out of it, except for almost being taken down myself. I was going to have to be a whole lot smarter in the future if I wanted to carry out my plans, not to mention keeping myself alive.

I waited another hour until full dark before I left the cover of the trees. Even then I walked warily. I followed Holzer's path over the ridge, ready for anything, but he really was gone. When I reached my car, I stood in the shadows for about fifteen minutes, watching and listening, but again, there was nothing. It looked safe, so I finally got in the car and drove home.

I parked one block over when I got home. I didn't want to drive right up to my house, or even drive by it. My instincts hadn't been too good lately. It was time to start being seriously cautious. I walked in the shadows until I reached a point where I could see both the house and the street outside. It all seemed quiet. I waited five minutes to make sure and was rewarded with the sight of a brief flare of light from a parked car halfway down the block. Someone sitting inside had just lit a cigarette. I watched until another car drove down the street. The glare of its headlights illuminated the interior of the parked car. There was no one visible inside. Whoever it was had ducked down in the seat as the car went by. It wasn't a kid waiting for his date, that was for sure. Holzer, maybe? Hard to say.

I waited for him to duck down again as another car passed; then I sprinted across the street and took cover four cars back. I clutched my Walther in my hand and wormed my way toward his car, stomach brushing the ground, until I reached the rear. The man behind the wheel finished his cigarette and tossed it backward out the window without bothering to put it out. It landed on my hand, burning me slightly. I waited ten minutes until another car came up the street. As it passed, I straightened up and came up to the window. I caught him just as he was straightening up after the car passed by. The gun went into his ear.

"If you so much as twitch, your brains are going to be part of the upholstery."

He opened his mouth, and a sort of squeak came out. "Jason, is that you?"

It was Becker from homicide. "What the fuck are you doing up here?" I asked, almost squeaking, myself. The adrenaline was still flowing, and the relief of the anticlimax was making my voice break. Becker hadn't moved a muscle, but his eyes were almost twisted out of his head with trying to make eye contact with me.

"Jason, take the gun out of my ear. Please."

It was a temptation to let him think I was totally gone and that he was one bare instant from death, but desperation makes people do funny things. I pulled the gun back. "What are you doing here?" I repeated, a little more calmly.

"Volter. It was Volter's idea. He wants an eye kept on you." Now that the gun was out of his ear, Becker was rapidly regaining his composure. "Where the hell have you been, anyway?"

"Out. And now I'm in. I'm going inside my house, and I'm going to sleep, and you can tell Volter if he wants an eye kept on me he ought to hire a real cop."

I was too relieved to be mad, really. I also realized that by stationing Becker outside my house, Volter was actually doing me a favor. I could sleep soundly tonight. It's not everyone who gets his own personal bodyguard.

TWELVE

I slept until almost noon. Becker was still parked a little way down the street. I hoped the prick had been there all night without any relief. I was feeling pretty down. Everything had been going so smoothly, I thought. Now what the fuck was I going to do?

I sat down with coffee and a cigarette to think, but the phone rang. Dave Warren was on the other end.

"Hi, Jase. How's it going?" he said.

"So-so. Yourself?"

"Getting by. Volter said he'd been by to see you."

"He saw me."

"He said you didn't want to talk to him. Any particular reason?"

"Just don't much feel like talking these days."

"Yeah. Well, Volter's assigned Fat Eddie to me."

"Can't think of a better man."

"I'm going to give it my best shot, you know. I'm going to do my best to hang it on you, Jase. You'd do the same if it were me."

"No, I wouldn't, Dave. That's the difference between us."

"Bullshit."

"Whatever. Anyway, I'd wish you luck, but it wouldn't be sincere."

"If I'd had any luck, I wouldn't be on this case." There was a tone of tired resignation in his voice. "Christ, Jason, why did you have to do it? We would have got him, you know. Sooner or later."

"Well, now you don't have to worry about it."

"No, now I've got to worry about you."

"I appreciate the concern," I said dryly.

"You shouldn't have done it, Jase."

"There are a lot of things in my life I probably shouldn't have done."

"Haven't we all? See you," he said, and hung up.

I picked up my coffee and put Dave out of my mind. I needed to concentrate on what I was going to do. Allred, first, that much was clear. Holzer was tricky, and I needed time to work out a suitable plan on him. My last one hadn't gone so well. Allred might be tricky too, but I didn't think he was street smart like Holzer. It should be a lot easier to take Allred down. Besides, I wanted Holzer last anyway, just him and me. Fat Eddie had been nothing but a psycho. Allred wouldn't have had the guts to act alone. Holzer was the driving force. I wanted him to worry about what was happening a while longer.

Allred wasn't going to be all that easy, though. He would be doubly on guard now, and getting to him posed a problem. I didn't think he would ask for police protection. As far as he knew, I was the only one who had made the connection between him and the murdered women yet, but he might well have hired a couple of private bodyguards. His house would be well secured, and he wouldn't be alone too often. I had to take him off guard, when he felt safe.

I started to get an idea. I turned it over in my mind for a while. It was crazy. I was being dumb to even consider it. It was too far out. It would never work. I decided to give it a try.

I drove down to the 7-Eleven, picked up a pack of Pall Malls, and placed a call to Allred's office from the phone outside. I didn't even glance at Becker, who had followed me down to the store. As I picked up the phone, I saw him make a notation in his surveillance log, but he didn't try coming close enough to overhear me. He knew better.

"Good morning, Allred and Young," came the familiar voice of the receptionist. By now my voice as well might sound familiar, so I changed it. Unless someone knows you well, it's not that difficult to disguise your voice over the phone. Most people overdo it, trying to put on an accent or use a strange voice, which completely defeats the purpose. It just sounds like someone trying to disguise his voice and makes the person on the other end listen all the more carefully. All you need to do is adjust the natural pitch of your voice slightly and alter the natural rhythm of your speech pattern. It works every time.

"My name is Kauffman, Steven Kauffman," I said. "I need to see about retaining Mr. Allred."

"Is this civil or criminal, sir?"

"It's a criminal case. Real criminal. I need to see him as soon as I can."

"Mr. Allred is busy all day today, but he does have some time free tomorrow afternoon at four, if that would be convenient?"

"That'll do just fine," I assured her. "I'll be there."

A little before six I got in my car. Becker had been replaced by Fletcher Choames, who pulled out behind me, right on my tail. I felt almost sorry for him. Choames was the guy who always managed to screw up, but this time it wouldn't really be his fault. An open tail, where you just want to keep track of someone, is easy to do, but it's also easy to shake.

I didn't get fancy, I just used the oldest dodge in the book, slowing down when I reached a busy intersection with the light turning yellow, and then punching it just as the light turned red. I scooted across to the accompaniment of blaring horns from outraged drivers, but Choames was taken totally by surprise, trapped at the intersection. I could see him in the rearview mirror, looking depressed. I could just hear him trying to explain how he lost me in five minutes. At the next cross street I turned left, out of sight, and made for downtown Salt Lake. I was headed for Blink's Tavern.

Blink's Tavern isn't a tavern at all; it's a tattoo parlor. Blink was an old-time con who had been around forever. He made his money these days tattooing street kids too stupid to know better and fencing whatever they could steal on the side. Blink also happened to be an informant. A few years ago he was looking at one to fifteen at the Point, and turned one of the biggest dealers in the city to get out from under it. He wasn't real fond of me, but he was reliable, because I owned him. I still had the evidence to send him away, and he knew it.

I parked around the back of the shop. Blink always came out the back door after locking up. I'd waited there ten minutes when he appeared. Blink was fatter than ever. He must have weighed almost as much as Fat Eddie, but at five foot seven the effect wasn't quite the same. He sloshed and rippled when he walked. Street lore had it that he was born with two stomachs. It might even have been true. I waited until he was through with the door and honked my horn. He looked up cautiously and then waddled over to the car.

"Oh, fuck," he said, when he saw who it was.

"Blink, is that any way to greet an old friend?" I opened the passenger door. "Get in." He sighed and slid onto the seat. The car sagged as he sat down.

"What do you want, Coulter?"

"Just a little favor. Nothing that'll cost you."

"What's in it for me?"

"How about you staying out of prison a while longer?"

"Shit, man, how long you gonna hold that over me?"

"Take heart, Blink. The statute of limitations will run out in a couple of years and then you can tell me to fuck off. Unless of course I catch you in the meantime fencing the crap you buy off your street punk friends."

"I don't fence stuff. I'm legit."

"Right. And I'm the Holy Virgin. Let's cut the bullshit. I don't have the time."

"So?"

"I want a tattoo."

He looked at me in astonishment and bellowed a laugh that shook his jowls. "You're shitting me."

"Not a real tattoo. Something that will pass as real for a couple of hours. Something that comes off."

"Oh, you mean kiddie tattoos. Sure, I do 'em all the time for juvvies who want to look cool but can't quite take the plunge."

"What do you use, special ink?"

"Nah. Pentel pens work the best. You'd be surprised how good they look, at least for a few days. Unless you wash." He looked at me inquiringly. "What, you gonna be a biker or something?"

I smiled slowly. "That really isn't any concern of yours, is it now?"

"Okay, okay. Just curious."

"Don't be."

"All right. Take it easy. Jesus." He wheezed heavily for a few moments. "Where do you want this tattoo, anyway?"

"Tattoos. Both arms. Shoulders too."

Blink squealed in protest. "Shit, Coulter, do you know how long that would take? To do all that? Half the fucking night, that's how long."

I smiled again and shrugged. "I guess we better get started then, hadn't we?"

Blink sat there sullenly, then muttered something and yanked open the car door. "Fuckin' cops," he whined, and opened up the door to the shop.

I stripped off my shirt and Blink got started. I have to give him credit; he was good. Starting on the left arm, he drew a snake coiling around, twisting up the length of my arm with an alternating pattern of green and red. I was surprised to see that he really took pains with it, and it took almost an hour. Then he covered the shoulder with a blue dragon.

"God, it's hot," he said, and started to pull off his shirt.

"Blink, no, don't do that," I pleaded. It was hard enough to sit next to him in the heat of the shop even with the shirt on. Blink was not someone who believed in regular bathing.

"Do what?"

I sighed. "Never mind. Let's get this over with."

I looked at him, repelled but fascinated. I had never realized just how fat he really was. Huge folds of skin and flesh overlapped each other, glistening and swaying gently. As he reached up to take my other arm, something fell out of one of the folds over his stomach. I reached over gingerly and lifted the fold away from his body, nauseated but unable to stop myself. About a half cup of cheerios dribbled out onto the floor. I shuddered. He must have spilled them last night lying in bed, watching TV and they had been trapped in the folds of fat. At least I hoped it was only last night. He reached down and brushed away a few that had remained, stuck to his skin. There were a couple that stuck to his fingers and he popped them into his mouth. I thought I was going to be sick.

He started working on the right arm, drawing an intricate series of satanic symbols: a devil's head, the pyramid with the eye, an upside-down crucifix, complete with figure, a six-pointed star with a goat's head in the middle, and right across the bicep, in large numerals, the number 666. He leaned back finally and surveyed his work critically.

"Aleister Crowley would have been proud," I said, looking at the arm in the mirror. Blink looked at me blankly. I didn't explain that Crowley was the father of modern-day occultists.

He smudged a couple of the drawings just a bit so they would look older than the rest, as if they had been done over a period of time, and finally was satisfied with the effect. I looked in the mirror, I couldn't tell the drawings from authentic tattoos.

"Not too shabby, eh?" he said. He was obviously proud of his work. This was a side of him I had never seen.

"I'm impressed," I said. "Now if you'll just

put your shirt back on, I'll be really impressed." I slipped on my own shirt and walked over to the door.

"Thanks," I said, my hand on the knob. "I really am impressed. You're an artist, Blink."

"Yeah, I am kind of, aren't I?"

"You still want to know what this is about?"

"Well, yeah, sure. I mean, this is pretty far out."

"Well, don't worry, you'll figure it out sooner or later. Somebody might even come by and ask you about it. And when you do figure it, you might just get the urge to drop a dime."

"You know me, Jason. I wouldn't do anything like that."

"No, of course not. But if you did happen to feel that urge . . ."

"I know, I know. I'll end up out at the joint."

I took my hand off the knob. "Noo . . . I don't think I'd bother with that. You know what I think I'd do? I think I'd just tell Big Willie exactly what went down when his brother took that fall last time. You know, just sort of lay the whole thing out for him."

"Hey, man, don't even joke about that."

"No joke, Blink."

"Fuck, Coulter, you can't do that. I'd be dead in a week."

"I know."

He wiped the excess sweat off his face with his wadded-up shirt. "Hey, man, mellow out. I'm cool. I wouldn't say anything to anyone, you know that."

"Sure, Blink, I know that. Just a reminder, if

I take a fall, so do you. Only you won't be getting up again. Do you read me?"

"Yeah, yeah, I get you. It's cool. Don't worry."

"I'm not worried, Blink. Just explaining how things are."

I looked down again at the tattoos on my arms. "Nice job, Blink," I said, *"Real* nice job."

No one from the department was in sight when I got back to my house. Either they'd given up the idea of a tail, or they were going to try to do it right next time. I spent the rest of the night with a bottle of gin and a pile of old jazz albums, thinking of my life and how things had been. And about how things might have been. I go through that every once in a while, but it was worse this time, with Jennifer and all. After a while I managed to work through the self-pity. What was, was; what is, is, and all that crap. It takes me a long time to get to that point, and it doesn't ever last for more than a day, but at least I was able to get some sleep that night.

As soon as I woke up I took my coffee outside to the front step and lit a morning cigarette. Still no sign of anyone. My neighbor, an old geezer who lived directly opposite me, was out working on his lawn. He waved over a greeting when he saw me. He must have been eighty-five if he was a day, but he could still get around pretty good. He always kept his lawn and flower bed immaculate and couldn't understand why I didn't. I used to let my lawn go until it resembled a miniature jungle. It wasn't just that I was lazy, which I was; it was more that I didn't like the look of the carefully trimmed and edged plot of green that seemed to be everyone else's pride and joy. Stony hated it too. When the grass was short, there just wasn't enough cover. He would crouch down on the quarter-inch grass, trying to flatten himself into the earth, looking about as inconspicuous as a hard-core biker at a Mormon wedding. He wasn't an inconspicuous cat at the best of times. He would glance furtively from side to side, realizing that he was exposed and out of place. Sometimes I knew exactly how he felt.

I did have to start mowing the lawn, however, when I came home one day to find that my eighty-five-year-old neighbor had come over and done it for me. I guess he just couldn't stand looking at it anymore. He never said anything to me about it, but from that time on I made it a point not to let the grass get too high. I didn't want to be responsible for him having a heart attack while he was out mowing my lawn. If he keeled over mowing his own lawn, that was his business.

I noticed Stony over in the bushes intently stalking something. It was like one of those nature programs they show on TV, where there's always some tiger or something lying in wait, and the antelope blithely wanders closer and closer. The tiger springs; the antelope darts frantically away, and the chase is on. There are two reactions to this scene, depending on who's watching. One is to automatically yell, "Run!" and the other is to shout, "Get 'em!" It all depends on your viewpoint.

With a quick rush Stony dashed out of the bushes and pounced. There was a flurry of squawks, and then he came racing across the street with his trophy in his mouth, thrown back across one shoulder. He had managed to catch a large jay and the damn thing was nearly as big as he was. It wasn't giving up easily, either. It was squawking and beating its wings, trying to get free. Four or five other jays which had seen the assault took to the air and started dive-bombing Stony as he galloped home. One of them actually hit him hard enough to make him lose his balance, along with his grip on the bird he was carrying. As soon as it was free, it swooped off up into the air, apparently none the worse for the experience. The rest of the jays continued their attack, shrieking louder than ever, now with an unmistakable sound of triumph in their cries. Stony took it for a moment and then, totally baffled at the turn of events, flattened his ears and slunk under the cover of a parked car. I must admit my sympathies in the affair lay with the birds.

The jays gave it up after a few more half-hearted swoops at his hiding place, and a minute later, Stony came strolling out from under the car, as nonchalant as always, not a hair out of place. He looked at me suspiciously, not sure whether I had witnessed the debacle.

"Yes, I saw the whole thing," I assured him. "You're a wimp."

He licked one paw and sauntered off, probably in search of something more his size, like a hummingbird.

The rest of the morning was spent disassembling and cleaning the Beretta I had brought back from San Francisco. A .25 is a funny weapon. It looks more like a toy than a real gun, and the rounds are so small that it's hard to believe they could do any serious harm, but it's deadly all the same. Unobtrusive, easily concealed, and above all, quiet. A gun much favored by professional hit men.

In the movies hit men always use a silencer. The gun goes *phfft, phfft,* and the target drops. In real life it doesn't work that way. There is no such thing as a silencer. "Noise suppressor" would be a better term. With a silencer a shot doesn't sound like a shot, but it still makes noise. It sounds like a heavy book being dropped on a table. Most of the noise of a gunshot comes from the gases expanding out of the barrel, which is why, of course, you can't silence a revolver like you can an automatic. When a revolver barrel is covered, the gases simply escape from around the cylinder.

You don't need anything mechanical and complicated for a silencer, either. A one-liter plastic Coke bottle is as effective as the most expensive hardware. You just slip the opening over the end of the muzzle and fire through the bottom of the bottle. The only drawback is that it's a one-time shot, so to speak.

But there is another silencer just as effective, and always available—the human body. A .25 auto pressed up hard against the chest makes less noise than a cap gun. It can't even be heard in the next room if the door is closed. That's one of the things that makes it so useful.

I put the Beretta in my pocket and went

down into the basement. After digging around awhile, I found what I was looking for, a costume-store wig that I had used a couple of times in the past to good effect. Then a sleeveless black tank top, and a look in the mirror to see if it was going to work. The wig looked phony to me, so I added a Peterbilt cap, the kind with a bill that guys in bars wear to show that they're truckers and not Burger King cooks. I liked the effect. With the long hair and a two-day growth of beard, I didn't look much like Jason Coulter, anyway. I didn't look like anyone I'd really care to know. I looked like half the people I'd arrested. I couldn't very well wear gloves to Allred's office, so I'd have to be careful about what I touched.

The clock read two-fifteen, time to get started. I threw a long-sleeved windbreaker over my shoulder and drove around aimlessly for a while, watching for tails. There weren't any, but I twisted through a subdivision just to make sure. The lack of tail bothered me. It didn't make sense to put someone on me and then just give up. I got out and crawled under the car, and, sure enough, there was a motion detector, nestled up under the rear bumper. They were still following me, only from about six blocks away. I removed it and placed it carefully by the side of the road. I didn't want to break it. Those things are expensive.

I still didn't feel easy. It was too simple; Dave would have done better than that. After a moment's thought I lifted the hood and peered into the engine compartment. It took me a minute to spot the second one, hidden carefully under the water pump, attached by a strong magnet. Another old ploy, the easy-find, hard-find, but sometimes the old tricks work the best. This one I removed gently and placed on the seat next to me.

I pulled out of the subdivision and stopped at the McDonald's up on 21st South. I picked up the bug and gently affixed it under the bumper of a Jeep Cherokee sitting in the lot there. Dave was going to be pissed when he finally caught up to them. Then I headed downtown.

When I got downtown, I parked in the Crossroads Mall. The mall had worked for me last time, and I didn't see any reason to alter things. I reflected wryly that I was developing an M.O. Criminals stick to what they know, what they're comfortable with, what has worked for them in the past. I had a moment's uneasiness when I realized that. It's one of the ways people get themselves caught.

It took me about ten minutes of easy walking to reach the Judge Building, which housed the law office of Allred and Young. I took the elevator up to the seventh floor. There was one other passenger, a pretty young blonde. She looked at me and quickly looked away, not happy to be riding in the same elevator. I ignored her but saw the surreptitious glances she kept casting at the tattoos on my arms. She seemed especially fascinated by the snake. When she got off at the fifth floor, I noted with satisfaction that she hadn't once looked at my face.

The Allred and Young law office was down the hall and around the corner from the elevator. It was just before three when I pushed open the office door and looked around. There were several people in the office, waiting to see either Allred or his partner, Burton Young. I swaggered over to the receptionist's desk.

"Can I help you, sir?" she asked, looking up.

It was the secretary with the cheerful voice. Somewhat to my disappointment, I saw she was middle-aged and slightly frumpy. She knew her job, though. If she was put off at all by my appearance, it didn't show. Allred must have a lot of clients whose appearance was as bad as mine, if not worse. It may not take all kinds to make a world, but it certainly does to make a legal practice.

"I got an appointment to see Mr. Allred," I told her. "Name's Kauffman."

"Oh, you're Mr. Kauffman? Mr. Allred is still with a client, but if you'd like to take a seat, he'll be with you in just a few minutes."

I grunted and sat down across the room. I crossed my legs, picked up a copy of the *Deseret News*, and turned to the sports page, holding up the paper so it shielded my face.

In about ten minutes the door to Allred's office opened and he came into the outer office, laughing and joking with a young man who sported shoulder-length blond hair and a short beard, neatly trimmed. Probably a dope case. Allred had one arm around the boy's shoulders in a fatherly manner. He walked him to the outer door, said good-bye, and turned back to his secretary.

"Mr. Kauffman waiting to see you," said the secretary, motioning toward me.

Allred walked over to me and put out his

hand. He had a firm, manly handshake, well calculated to inspire trust. I didn't think he'd recognize me in my altered state. He'd only seen me before in a police setting, suit and tie, reasonably well-groomed and professional. He was also expecting to see a client, and people tend to see what they expect. The theory was sound, but I still had a moment of doubt that I could pull it off. I glanced into his eyes, looking for that telltale glint of recognition, but it wasn't there. He wasn't really looking at my face anyway. His attention was fixed on those beautiful and useful tattoos.

"Let's go to my office, why don't we?" he said, leading the way. He closed the door to his office behind us and sat down in a leather chair behind his desk. The desk was made of polished mahogany and was large enough so that I would have to lean across it to get at him. It must have cost five thousand dollars, another confidence-inspiring ploy, the trappings of a successful attorney. I took a seat on the other side of the desk and sprawled out in the chair. Allred looked at me with a slight expression of distaste mixed with puzzlement.

"Do I know you?" he asked suddenly.

"Yeah, you do," I agreed.

"I thought I did, but I can't quite place you."

"That's a shame, counselor, really a shame. Maybe you should pay more attention to people."

"What are you talking about?" He was beginning to feel the first faint stirrings of alarm. I eased the Beretta out of my pocket and pointed it at him. His face tightened, but he kept himself under control.

"Now what exactly is going on?" he said, voice low-pitched and reasonable, eyes riveted on the gun.

"It's simple enough," I replied. "It has to do with a woman. It has to do with sickness. It has to do with murder. It has to do with a guy named Fat Eddie and a guy name Holzer. And right now it has to do with a guy named Julian Allred. Juley to his friends, *you motherfucker.*"

I hissed out the last words with a hatred I hadn't known was in me. Allred's well-manicured hands were twitching on the desk. I could see them smoothly stroking Jennifer, just before she died. He wouldn't have killed her himself. He would have walked away and turned his back. It might even have made him a little queasy. I felt an all-consuming fury. I didn't just want to kill this man. I wanted to physically beat his face in until he was no longer recognizable as a human being.

It must have been in my voice. He looked at me, really looked at me for the first time.

"Coulter!"

I nodded and his face twisted up with fear.

"Now wait a minute . . ." he started. I lunged across the desk, pulled him toward me, shoved the gun into his chest, and pulled the trigger twice. The shots were muffled, almost inaudible. Allred gave a convulsive twitch and staggered up out of his chair, gasping, making croaking, bubbling sounds. I was afraid someone would hear him, and I shuffled quickly around to the other side of the desk. He was now gagging, bent over in pain. I turned him around, grabbing his throat in the crook of my arm and squeezing the carotid arteries. It was another technique the police department had so thoughtfully provided me with. Allred tried feebly to fight me off, but he could barely raise his arms. In three seconds, as the blood stopped flowing to his brain, he went limp. Two seconds later he went into convulsions, and I had to drag him away from the desk to prevent him from banging into it and making more noise. The convulsions went on for at least ten seconds, powerful and violent. He quivered noiselessly on the thick carpet a few more seconds. Then his entire body gave a final shudder and was still.

I was panting, gasping for air out of all proportion to the struggle, which had lasted just a little more than fifteen seconds. There was no indication that anyone in the next room had heard a thing. There was blood on my wrist from where I had been holding him, and I wiped it off absently on one of the leather chairs. I was starting to feel slightly sick to my stomach. My rage had evaporated. I didn't look at Allred, crumpled up on the rug. I walked over to the door that led to the outer office, paused to get my voice under control, and opened it. Standing in the doorway, I was clearly visible to people in the outer office, but they couldn't see into the room. "Thanks," I called back over my shoulder. "I'll stay in touch."

I gave a friendly wave toward the now-dead lawyer, nodded at the secretary, and walked casually into the corridor outside. I figured I'd have at least five minutes before anyone checked on him, but something must have made the secretary nervous. I had hardly closed the door behind me when I heard a scream from the office. I ignored the elevator and ducked into the stairwell, almost breaking my neck as I took the steps four and five at a time. When I reached ground level, I slipped on the windbreaker to cover the tattoos, rolled up the wig and the cap, stuffed them under one arm, and strolled through the lobby. Fifty feet from the building entrance is an alley that cuts through the block. The wig and cap went into the first dumpster I came across, and the Beretta, wiped carefully on my shirt, went into the next one after that. As I came out of the alley, I saw a black-and-white hustling down the street toward Allred's office.

All I had to do now was make it home, shower and shave, and I was home free. I circled around until I reached the mall, not exactly nervous but still looking around guardedly, when I saw someone I recognized. It was Brian, Jennifer's ex. I turned my face away, but he wasn't looking toward me anyway. He was staring at the ground, lost in his own world. In one hand was a package wrapped in white paper. In the other he was carrying something that sent a chill through my whole body. It was something from Earth Works, the garden shop on the first level, something ordinary and prosaic, nothing that should have been any cause for alarm. It seemed to shimmer with a life of its own. It filled me with horror. It was a shiny brand-spanking-new shovel.

THIRTEEN

Sometimes you understand things instantly, beyond thought, beyond logic. Maybe it's the subconscious, putting together all the seemingly trivial clues. Maybe there really is some kind of psychic awareness. It doesn't matter what the mechanism is. I looked at Brian and I *knew* with the certainty of death.

Everything had fit together so perfectly, and had been so wrong. Allred. Fat Eddie. Holzer. The pickup truck. The girl on State Street, the one they killed. All those other missing women, still missing, forever gone. Jennifer's empty car. There had never been a doubt in my mind, but I had been totally off-track. It wasn't them at all; it was him. It was Brian who had killed her, and now he was going to bury her with his shiny new shovel.

I didn't know what to do. I hung back and followed him as he strolled around the mall. He didn't seem to be in any hurry. I started to have doubts. Maybe I really was over the edge. A lot of people buy shovels, for a lot of reasons. I kept trying to study his face without getting too close, looking for a clue, trying to see something in him that would convince me I was right. He stopped at a booth near the escalator and had an orange drink. He looked as normal as could be.

Finally he left the mall, going straight to the second level parking terrace. I followed him out and watched as he got into his car. Only, he didn't get into a car. He got into a dark brown pickup truck.

I almost let him get away. I just stood there, staring in disbelief. The whole world was too bright. The pickup was too sharp, etched into my vision. Everything seemed tilted, off-kilter. I stood and stared.

Then he started up the truck, rousing me from my trance. I sprinted down one level to my car and got to the mall exit just behind him. He drove slowly around the downtown area for what seemed like hours, looking straight ahead the whole time, which made following him easy. Finally he turned on Fifth South and onto the freeway entrance, heading south and then east, toward the foothills. He still wasn't paying attention to things around him. We ended up southbound on Wasatch Drive, and I could hear Dave's words in my ears, words I hadn't paid any attention to at the time. "Money, a cabin up at Brighton, the whole bit." I almost sobbed with anger and frustration. Why hadn't I been smarter? It was so obvious now. Brian had taken her up to his cabin. If I'd thought of it sooner, maybe I could have saved her.

A thought struck me. Maybe she wasn't dead after all. He wouldn't kill her right away; he would hold her at the cabin for a while until all his sick fantasies were played to the hilt. Maybe the shovel was for preparation, not for cleanup.

By the time we made the turn up Big Cottonwood to Brighton, my mind had flipped back and forth at least ten times about whether or not Jennifer was still alive. I made myself stop thinking about it. I was going to know one way or the other soon, and I needed all my concentration.

Brighton isn't really a town. It's more a collection of vacation houses centered around a five-mile loop that runs around the resort. I stayed a few hundred yards behind Brian and let a couple of other cars pass me. When his truck pulled off onto a long driveway, I drove past and parked about fifty yards down the road. I made my way through the woods, parallel to the driveway, and came up on the cabin from the back side. It was small and comfortable looking, a freshly painted white with blue trim around the eaves and windows, almost "cutesy." There were sliding doors in the back, covered with drapes, leading onto a small patio. A disused barbecue grill lay rusting in one corner. Brian's pickup was parked by the front door.

I crept up to the back by the doors and listened. Nothing. I tried them cautiously, but they were locked. I tried to look inside through the small crack between the glass of the doors and the inside drapes. I could see only part of the room, a stone fireplace, and the corner of what looked like a dining room table. Brian was sitting at the table, or at least I assumed it was him. All I could see was a pair of hands. He was doing something with a piece of rope. I crossed over to the other side of the window where I could see the other edge of the room, and there she was.

Jennifer was lying facedown on the floor, turned partly to the wall. Her hands were tied behind her with wire. She still had her halter top on, but she was naked from the waist down. It looked like her jeans had been rolled up and placed under her head. She wasn't moving. She looked dead, but I couldn't be sure. Then I saw it, and my hope died. Her neck seemed to be at an awkward angle to the rest of her body, and the back of her head was dark with clotted blood. Flies buzzed around it. A metallic taste filled my mouth. I was too late, after all.

There was a faint sound of a chair scraping away from the table. A second later Brian came into view and stood over her. He held a piece of rope in one hand and a bread knife in the other. He crouched over her body, bouncing gently on his heels, crooning. Then he raised his voice and began talking in a bright, cheerful tone, the way some adults speak to children they don't know very well. I could just make out his voice now, catching about half the words, blurred through the glass.

"Poor Jenny . . . now look at . . . you

shouldn't have ... never ..." He was rocking back and forth. He placed the knife carefully on the floor and slid his hand between her legs, caressing her in an obscene parody of tenderness. I thought I could see blood there, too.

It was so sick I was paralyzed, barely comprehending. I had encountered the face of madness, bubbling out in a poisonous stew. I wanted to run away, just forget I had ever seen this. At that moment I could have gladly killed Brian, but I don't think I could have brought myself to touch him. They say the things you imagine are worse than anything you can actually experience. They aren't. This particular reality was beyond anyone's imagining.

He took his hand from between her legs and started stroking her hair, brushing away the flies. With the other hand he picked up the knife. Then he grabbed her hair and pulled her head back. I could hear him distinctly for the first time.

"Time for the final dance, Jenny," he said. As he pulled her head back, she moaned.

I can't remember any conscious thought. All I know is that I was throwing the barbecue through the glass doors and screaming at the top of my lungs. I crashed through the door, getting tangled up in the drapes and tearing them off the curtain rod. I ripped at them frantically. Brian, still crouched on his heels, was gaping up at me, a look of bewilderment on his face. He hadn't yet come out of his little fantasy. It took him only a second, though. He uttered a strangled cry and came at me with the knife. He didn't hold it like an amateur either, but like someone who has had special forces training, haft first, blade laid back along the forearm. I had misjudged him. It flashed through my mind that I had been misjudging and misunderstanding just about everything lately.

He looped a shot toward my head, and when I instinctively ducked, turned the blade over and came up with a backhand slash. He had misjudged things a little himself, though. I still had the drapes in my hand, and as the blade came up, I caught the blade in the folds and grabbed his arm. I clamped on tight with my right hand and jammed my left palm under his nose. We struggled together, panting, until he loosened his grip on the knife slightly and I managed to twist it away. It fell to the floor, and he jumped back, breathing loudly. We stared across the room at each other. Then he spun and bolted for the door. I went after him, not to catch him, but to make sure he wasn't going to his truck for another weapon. He didn't stop. He kept on down the driveway toward the main road.

I ran back inside and knelt down next to Jennifer. She was trying to sit up. She was conscious, but didn't recognize me. I supported her and felt the pulse at her throat. It was strong and even, a reassuring sign. I untwisted the wire around her wrists, cutting my thumb in the process. She started rubbing her arms where the wire had cut in, looking at me with a puzzled air. Then her eyes cleared, and she looked into my face.

"Jason," she whispered. Her voice got

stronger. "Jason," she repeated. She tried to smile, but it didn't work very well. She reached out slowly and held on to me. "Oh, God, I thought I was dead. I knew I was dead. Oh, my God. Oh, Jason."

I held her next to me. I still couldn't believe she was alive. "It's okay," I said. "It's okay."

"How ... how did you find me? What happened to Brian? How did ..."

"Later. We've got to get you out of here. Can you walk?"

"I think so." She started to get up, then slumped back down. "No, I guess I can't. I'm sorry."

There was no way I was going get my car and leave her there, even for five minutes. I managed to get her jeans back on her and carried her down the road to where my car was parked. Several cars passed us and looked at us curiously, but no one stopped.

"Are we going home now?" she asked plaintively.

"Hospital."

"I'd rather go home. I don't feel that bad now. Really I don't."

"Your head says different. You need X rays."

I headed toward St. Mark's, the best hospital in the valley, and as I pulled up to the Emergency Room entrance I suddenly realized I had a small problem. As soon as the staff got a look at Jennifer and her injuries, they were going to notify the police. Dave would be right on it. That was fine with me, but I still had a bunch of tattoos under my windbreaker, and that wasn't.

I left Jennifer in the car and went into the E.R., pushing aside some people at the admitting desk who were asking about insurance forms.

"There's a seriously injured woman in my car," I said, pointing out through the doors. "Head injury, I don't know what else." As I said, it was a good hospital. The nurse didn't waste any time questioning me. She called a couple of aides with a stretcher and they hastened out to the car. Only then did she ask me what happened. I showed her my identification and told her that the woman had been attacked and that I had found her. A badge works wonders sometimes in avoiding embarrassing questions.

"Would you notify Detective Dave Warren, Salt Lake City Police?" I asked, leaning toward her over the counter. I owed him that much. "The woman's name is Jennifer Lassen. Also, is there a doctor's lounge I could borrow a few minutes to clean up? I'm covered with blood under this windbreaker." I gestured apologetically.

"Of course," she said, leading me to a doorway halfway down the hall. Inside was a small lounge and bathroom, complete with shower. I grabbed a towel hanging on the rack, stripped quickly and jumped in. In five minutes there wasn't a trace of color on me, only the glow of a freshly scrubbed body.

I hung around the desk while they were getting Jennifer cleaned up and ready to take down to X ray, and before too long Dave walked through the door. He grabbed me by the arm.

"Is it true, Jase? She's alive?"

"It's true. Remember Brian, her boyfriend? It was him. He kidnapped her, took her up to his cabin in Brighton. I really don't know much more about it."

"Is she okay?"

"I think so. I hope so."

"I can't believe it," he said. "I can't believe she's alive."

The nurse who had showed me to the lounge walked by and interrupted. "Did you get cleaned up okay?"

I nodded my thanks, but Dave put a hand on her arm. "Cleaned up?"

"The detective here. He needed to get cleaned up, so I let him use the shower in the doctors' lounge."

"I really appreciate it," I told her, looking at Dave. He turned to me as she walked away.

"Since when do you take showers in hospitals?" He looked at me thoughtfully. "Why not wait until you get home? What's going on, Jase?"

I shrugged. "You want to hear about Jennifer?" I asked, changing the subject. "Brian is still out there somewhere running around, you know."

"Yeah, of course, tell me what happened. How did you get on to him, anyway?"

"It's kind of weird. I was just driving along when this pickup pulls up at the light, with Brian driving . . ."

"I didn't know he owned a pickup."

"Yeah, me neither. That's why we missed it. So it started me thinking, and I . . ."

Dave suddenly slapped his forehead with his

hand. "Of course. The tattoos. It was the god-damn tattoos," he said. "You didn't have time until now to clean them off. I'll be god-damned. What did use for them, Jason? Some kind of special ink?"

"Dave, what are you talking about?"

"Don't bullshit me, Jason. I don't expect you to roll over for me, but don't feed me that 'what are you talking about?' crap. I figured you were behind it, but it didn't connect that you actually did it yourself. Slick, real slick." He held up his hand. "And spare me the 'did what?' will you?"

I shrugged again. "Listen, you want to hear about Jennifer or don't you?"

"Jesus Christ, Jason. It was bad enough when you were going around pulling this Death Wish stuff, but you got the wrong peo-ple, for God's sake. They didn't have anything to do with it."

"You'd feel better about things if they'd re-ally killed her?"

"Don't give me that. She doesn't have any-thing to do with this, and you know it. You blew it. You fucked it up, Jase. You've been going around blowing away the bad guys, only it turns out you got the wrong ones. Jesus fucking Christ."

"You bought it, too."

"Yeah, I bought it, but I didn't kill anyone."

He walked a few steps away and raised his hands in frustration. I realized that what he was angriest about was that the happy ending and the rescue of the damsel in distress was seriously marred by the fact he still had to do his best to put me away for killing Allred and

Fat Eddie. My killing them was bad enough, but to find out that it wasn't even necessary was just more than he could take.

After a few minutes he got control of himself and came back. "Okay, Jason," he finally said, "we'll drop it for now. What happened with Jennifer?"

I ran down the whole thing for him, except for exactly where I had been when I first caught sight of Brian. He listened intently. When I'd finished, he had a few questions, but pretty much just accepted my account. There wasn't any reason for me to be lying, not about this. He guessed Brian would be picked up in a couple of days at most.

Jennifer was back from X ray and the news was good—a slight concussion, but no fracture. They wanted to keep her overnight, but she was feeling stronger and walking unaided and didn't want to stay. After extracting a promise from me to wake her up a couple of hours after she first went to sleep, they let her go home. It's not uncommon after a head injury to pass out again a few hours later if there's blood leaking into the brain, causing it to swell with pressure. If it's going to happen, it's mostly likely to after you lie down for a while and sleep. Sometimes you never wake up again, so it's a good idea to have someone keep an eye on you.

Dave was still angry, but he walked us out to the car. "For her sake, stay home for a change," he said. "Take care of her, will you?"

Jennifer collapsed into the bed as soon as we were home. I watched her sleep for a while, marveling at my luck. It had been so close. Now it was going to be all right. Dave would do his best on the cases, but he wasn't going to break them. I wasn't sure if he really wanted to, anyway.

I tried to think about what I had done, but I wasn't ready. I wondered how Jennifer would take it when she found out. I wasn't ready to think about that either. I'd killed two people because I thought they were responsible for her death, and they hadn't been. But they were killers, both of them. If it hadn't been for Jennifer, I wouldn't have done anything about them. You can't go around killing everyone who deserves to die, no matter how strongly you feel. That way lies madness. But you can and should deal with those who strike against you and the ones you love. I didn't feel happy about the situation, but there wasn't much I could do about it now. A lot of people believe that all things happen the way they are meant to happen, anyway. I can't quite buy that, but it is a comforting thought.

After a couple of hours I shook Jennifer gently by the shoulder. No response. I panicked and shook her almost violently. She came awake in an instant, fear on her face. Then she saw me and relaxed, stretching out toward me. I took her in my arms.

"God, my head hurts," she said.

"I'm not surprised. Go back to sleep."

She put her head on the pillow and was asleep again in a minute. I disengaged myself slowly and slipped out of the bedroom. It had been a hell of a day. It was hard to believe that only hours ago I had thought Jennifer dead.

This afternoon Allred had been greeting clients. Brian had been buying a shovel, and I had been coldly plotting death. I wanted to go to sleep myself, pull the covers over my head and blot everything out. But not yet. There was still Holzer. God knows what he thought had been going on. He must have seen me as a cop who had gone around the bend. He would be taking it all very personally. There was no way to just call a truce. Kings X, we used to call it when I was a kid. He wouldn't quit until one of us was dead. I no longer had any stomach for the fight, but it wasn't my choice any longer. Maybe the best thing to do would be to just leave, take Jennifer and get out of town.

My thoughts, as usual, were interrupted by the ringing of the phone.

"Jason?"

"Brenda?"

"Yeah, it's me."

"How you doing? They let you out of jail okay?"

"Yeah, I got out the next morning. Thanks."

"No problem. So what kind of trouble are you in now?"

"What makes you think I'm in trouble?"

"You called, didn't you?"

"Well, yeah, but that doesn't always mean I'm in trouble. Maybe I just felt like calling."

"Brenda."

"Hey, maybe I just wanted to do you a favor, did you ever think about that?" She actually sounded hurt.

"Okay, sorry. My mistake. You're not in trouble."

"But I might be sometime."

I took the receiver away from my ear and stared at it for a second. "Brenda, what the fuck are you talking about?"

"I just thought if I did you a favor, you might remember it sometime."

"Don't I always?"

"No."

"Sure I do. But listen, kid, I don't know if I'm going to be able to do anything for you from now on."

"Yeah, I know. You been busy. I heard about it. Holzer was running his mouth down at the clubhouse."

"Oh? What did he say?"

"He says you killed Fat Eddie. He says you killed that lawyer friend of his, too. Hey, did you really do it?" she asked, a tone of something like awe creeping into her voice. "I mean, Jeez, you're a cop and everything, you know?"

"Brenda, would I do anything like that?"

"You did it. You really did it. Jeez."

"Weren't you going to tell me something?"

"Yeah, listen. Holzer had some sort of meeting with Chico and Blackie."

"Who's Blackie?"

"Blackie? He's the new second-in-command, you know, like if Chico's not around or something."

"Oh. What was the meet about?"

"That's the thing. They decided they're going to get you."

"Who?"

"The Pharaohs."

I laughed. "What, all of them?"

"Hey, this is no joke. They're going to take care of you before you can do anything else. They're bringing it up for a vote at the Friday night club meeting."

"That just doesn't make any sense. Chico's too smart to have anything to do with killing a cop, and certainly too smart to stick his neck out for Holzer."

"Holzer's a brother. it doesn't matter what he's like or what he's done. Don't you know anything about bikers? It's your brother, your bike, and your broad. In that order."

"It still doesn't figure."

"I can't help that; I'm just telling you what they're going to do."

"Yeah. Well, thanks for the warning."

"Sure. Hey, Jase?"

"Yeah?"

"Fat Eddie was real scum. Holzer's a nut case."

"They're your friends, Brenda, not mine."

She immediately got pissed. "Who I hang out with is my own fuckin' business, Coulter." Her tone softened a little. "I don't care what went on, whether you did it or not. Holzer's a prick. They're all pricks. They're all scum. Just be careful."

I hung up, bemused. Brenda going soft for a cop. Now I'd seen everything.

It still didn't make sense to me, but sometimes bikers don't. I couldn't discount what Brenda had told me. She'd been right too many times in the past. I sighed. Just when it looked like everything was straightening out, this stuff came up. If it hadn't been so serious it would have been funny. It was kind of funny anyway. A whole fucking biker club after me. What next?

An old cliché says cops and bikers are very much alike, just opposite sides of the same coin. It isn't really true, but like all clichés, there's something to it. Cops and bikers are closer in the way they think than either group is to John Q. Citizen. I could pretty much guess what was going on in Chico's mind.

Holzer must have sold him that I was a threat, not just to Holzer, but somehow to the entire club. Chico wouldn't want anything to do with killing a cop if there was any way out of it. A thin line of balance exists between bikers and cops. If the bikers don't go too far, the cops don't hassle them too bad. Every once in a while things get out of hand, there's a blowup, and then things get back to normal. But a biker club that puts out a contract on a cop is finished, no matter what the circumstances. Not one of them would be able to stick his nose out on the street without being arrested, on good charges or bad. In six months there wouldn't be a club. Chico was aware of that. He must be feeling desperate. If I could get to him and gave him an out, he'd take it.

Still, if it was true, I didn't care much for the odds. Holzer might be the worst, but he wasn't the only club member who was psycho, and there were a lot of members. If they really wanted me, they would get me, sooner or later. What makes bikers so dangerous is that they just don't care. They don't mind fighting, because they don't really care if they get hurt. They don't mind killing, because they don't really care if they get killed, either. At least, the younger ones don't. The older guys, guys like Chico, had survived long enough to get smart. That's why they ran things.

There were really only two things I could do. One was to pack up and move out of town. I didn't like that idea. Apart from the simple fact I didn't like being run out, bikers have long memories. The Pharaoh's had good relations with the Angels and Ravens on the West Coast, the Banditos down South, the Riders and Brother Speed, and probably a lot more clubs I hadn't even heard of. I'd spend the rest of my life looking over my shoulder. The other option was to talk Chico out of it, not an easy thing to do. And I had to do it now, before it came to a formal vote and they couldn't back out of it.

It was close to nine, getting dark out. Stony came in looking for dinner. I fed him, slipped my Walther under a windbreaker and looked in on Jennifer again. I was worried about leaving her alone, but I had to get this done before it was too late. She was breathing slowly and evenly. I gathered myself and headed down to the Pharaoh's clubhouse.

FOURTEEN

The clubhouse was on State Street. From the outside it looked ordinary, a dull brick structure built in the fifties, one of the few houses left in what is now mostly a business district. The Pharaohs liked it that way; there weren't any neighbors to complain about their numerous loud parties, or to provide interesting tales to the cops about what went on there late at night.

I wasn't too worried about going in. Even bikers don't take killing a cop lightly. They'd want some time to think it over. Still, you never know.

There were a couple of members sitting on the front porch, wearing colors. Both were standard issue bikers: beards, long hair, sheath knives, belts with wide buckles. Most of the time buckles like those were attached to a two-inch blade that slipped into a slit in the belt. They sell them at martial arts stores, with the understanding, of course, that no one will actually wear them.

One of the guys was blond and one dark, but otherwise they were interchangeable. I didn't recognize either of them. They looked at me incuriously as I parked, and then with growing interest as I walked directly up to the porch. The dark-haired one remained leaning against the porch railing, watching with lazy eyes. The other stepped in my way as I approached the door. It was closed, and I knew from my days in uniform that it was reinforced with steel plate on the inside, and secured with a police lock. No kicking-in-the-door type raids for these boys.

Blondie spoke as I walked up the steps. "Looking for someone, sport?"

"Chico."

"Who's Chico?"

"Who's Chico?" I mimicked. "Why don't you cut the crap and save us both a lot of time?"

Blondie looked over at his partner leaning against the railing. Dark Hair looked back and yawned. Blondie turned back to me.

"Ooh, a tough guy. Chico's not expecting anyone, sport. He don't like surprises. That's why I'm out here. Take a hike."

"The name's Coulter, sport. Jason Coulter. Why don't you tell Chico I'm here before we all do something stupid."

The name Coulter got a big reaction. Blondie took a step back, and Dark Hair scrambled to his feet. Apparently someone had been discussing me, all right. They dropped their studied casual manner.

"Wait here," said Blondie. Dark Hair stayed outside, watching me, a lot more carefully now.

It took less than a minute for Blondie to return.

"Inside," he said, jerking his head.

In the front room there were several more bikers, drinking beer, playing pool, and a few ladies sprawled on a big patterned rug in a back corner. I didn't see Brenda. We walked through into the kitchen. Chico was seated at a table, across from a guy I'd seen around occasionally, a heavyset guy with a thick black mustache and no beard. That must be Blackie. I noticed Chico had cut his hair short. He was beginning to look more like a businessman than the head of a biker club.

On the other side of the kitchen, in a chair next to the refrigerator, sat Jack Holzer. Chico took a swallow from a can of Coors he was holding.

"Mr. Coulter," he said sardonically. "So nice to see you." He took another swallow of beer. "You've got balls, I'll give you that." Holzer looked over at my escort.

"You search him?" he asked.

"Nobody said to."

"Shit."

Holzer leaned back in his chair in disgust. I immediately hooked my right hand in my belt to emphasize the point. There was no way I was going to be able to take all three of them if they decided to jump me, not in the confines of the kitchen, but it might make them hesitate.

"No problem," I said. "I'm not looking for trouble. Just here to talk."

"You can talk all you like once you're strung up by your balls," Holzer said.

"Cool it, Jack," said Chico. He set the beer can on the table. "You want to talk? Talk."

"Alone. One on one."

Blackie felt obliged to put in his two cents. "Uh-uh. We make the rules here, Coulter." Holzer shifted in his chair, and I turned slightly to keep an eye on him.

"Nervous, Coulter?" he drawled. I ignored him.

"This guy speaking for you now, Chico?" I said.

"Forget it, Coulter. That shit doesn't cut it with me. You want to talk, talk."

I wasn't going to get anywhere unless I could get Chico alone. As long as he was with Holzer and Blackie, he was going to keep posturing for them. He couldn't afford to let anyone in the club think that he wasn't in total control.

"Why don't we step outside for a minute, Chico?" I said. "You're not afraid to leave the boys, are you?"

"Why should I bother to get up from the table? I listen just as good sitting down."

I eased back against the corner of the room, leaning on my hands. The butt of the automatic against my hand was comforting. The wall felt soothing behind my back.

"No reason," I said. "Except that either I talk to you alone or I walk. And if I walk, the club is finished, no matter how it comes out. I just thought you might want to take five minutes of your time to save everything you've got."

Holzer rocked his chair forward and snapped out of it like a rubber man, reaching under his shirt. His hand was still under his shirt when I had the Walther out, pointed at the middle of his stomach.

"Don't do that, Jack," I said mildly.

Now that I had him, I didn't want him. I couldn't afford to shoot him anyway. I'd never make it out of there alive. Chico hadn't moved an inch.

"Okay, Coulter," he said. "You made your point." He turned to Holzer. "Put it up."

"Wait a minute," said Holzer, taking a step toward me. I lifted the gun, and then Blackie stepped between us. He and Holzer stared at each other for about five seconds, until Holzer shrugged, smiled, took his empty hand from under his shirt, and sat down again.

Chico unlocked the back door, which opened out into an alley behind the house, and motioned me through. I backed out, watching Holzer, and Chico followed. As soon as the door closed, I put the gun back in my belt and walked about twenty steps down the alley in silence. Chico stayed a few steps behind me. I wondered for a moment if I was going to get a bullet in the back of the head, after all. Then he came up alongside, still staying slightly behind and to the right of my gun hand.

"Good instincts," I told him. "You should have been a cop."

"I almost was, once."

"What happened?"

"Changed my mind."

"Probably for the best."

"Probably. So talk," he said.

"What line has Holzer been feeding you?"

"Uh-uh. You're the one who wants to talk."

"Okay, then. You're going to put a contract on me, I heard."

"Heard where?"

"Oh, you know. Around. You know what that means, killing a cop?"

"You ain't gonna be a cop much longer is what I hear."

"Don't be too sure. Doesn't matter anyway. They'll love an excuse to get rid of you. You know that."

"You don't leave me a whole hell of a lot of choice, Coulter."

"So says Holzer, right? That's trash. What did he tell you, that I was going to take you all down?"

"Something like that."

"And you buy it?"

"Fat Eddie bought it."

"Fat Eddie wasn't even a Pharaoh."

"Holzer is."

"Holzer's sitting at the kitchen table."

"What's your point, Coulter?"

"The point is that he's sold you some bogus goods. It's not the Pharaohs; it's him and me."

"He's a brother. You take him on, you take us all on."

"We're alone, Chico, so save the brotherhood speech. We've dealt with each other before. You don't like me, I don't like you. But you're not a psycho like Holzer. How many women has he killed, anyway?"

"That's his business." Chico hawked a glob of spit onto the pavement and looked over at me, almost defensive. "I just found out about that shit a couple of weeks ago."

"So what are you going to do, let one sick fucker pull down the whole club?"

"You trying to say something?"

"Just that there are other ways of taking care of the problem besides going after me. I'm not all that easy to take, Chico, and if you do, you're fucked even worse. What then?"

Chico chuckled deep in his throat. "That's what you call a ree-torical question, right?"

"Just leave it alone. Stall for a week. I'll be gone, and there won't be a problem. Until Holzer lands you in something else. It'll be over."

"If you think it'll be over, you don't know Holzer."

"Well, then, that's a problem between me and him, isn't it?"

Chico stopped and faced me in the darkness.

"Yeah," he said slowly. "I guess you could look at it that way." I could barely see the smile on his face in dim light. "Hey, Coulter, don't you think we're getting a little too old for this kind of shit?"

"I know I am. But that's the way things are. So . . . do we understand each other?"

"Oh, I think we do."

"You going to stay out of it?"

"I'll think on it," he said, and walked away in the darkness, back to the clubhouse.

* * *

I strolled back to my car, feeling pretty pleased with myself. The Pharaohs wouldn't be bothering me. Chico was smart enough to grasp that Holzer had become a big problem, and the best outcome, as far as he was concerned, would be for Holzer to get snuffed. He wouldn't do it himself. He'd wait for me to do it for him. If I could do it, fine. If it went down the other way around—well, that was okay too. Holzer would take the fall, be out of the way, and the Pharaohs wouldn't be involved. The cops would know it was just between me and Holzer. It wouldn't be like the Pharaohs had put out a contract.

Becker was back in front of the house when I got home. Volter couldn't seem to make up his mind about how to handle surveillance. This time Becker made sure that I could see it was him sitting there. I guess he didn't want a repeat of the last time.

Jennifer was still asleep, breathing easily. I undressed and slipped into bed beside her. For the first time in a week I relaxed, and slept the night away.

FIFTEEN

I woke up to the sound of the shower running. Things had come full circle. Girl in the shower. The smell of coffee drifting through the house. A second chance.

By the time Jennifer came out of the shower, I was in the kitchen with the coffee. I handed her a cup. She took a sip and looked at me over the rim. The towel wrapped around her hair was coming loose.

"How are you feeling?" I asked.

"Okay. A little weak, but okay." She smiled. "Pretty good, as a matter of fact. A lot better than yesterday at this time."

"I'll bet."

"I'm still a little paranoid, though. I keep looking out the window, thinking I'll see something. I saw someone sitting in a car across the street, and I kept thinking he was watching this house."

I got up and looked out the front window. Becker was gone, but he had been replaced by Phil Sandahl. "He is watching the house," I told Jennifer. "He's a friend of mine. Sort of."

"I don't understand. Why is he out there?"

"Finish your coffee. I guess there are some things we have to talk about. I'll be back in a few minutes."

"I strolled out in the morning light to where Phil sat waiting in his car. "Morning, Phil," I greeted him.

"Jason."

"You had your coffee yet?"

He held up a 7-Eleven cup, with the lid on tight and a swizzle stick straw poked through a little hole in the top. He was the only person I ever met who drank coffee through a straw. Years ago, as a patrolman, he got tired of spilling coffee in his lap every time there was an emergency call. He came up with the idea of a lid and straw. After about five years it got to be such a habit that he drank it like that even at his desk up in homicide. He took a lot of grief about it, but it didn't seem to bother him any. I don't know what he did when he was at home.

There was a morning paper in the back seat, and I pointed at it. "Mind if I take a look at that?"

"Be my guest." He handed the paper to me through the window. "Front page story. Prominent attorney murdered. Link between killing and previous murder suspected. Police department tight-lipped."

"Sounds exciting. Any leads?"

"Rumor has it that the case is about to be broken."

"Don't believe everything you hear, Phil."

I leaned against the car and read the account of Allred's shooting. It was fairly accurate, except for the description of the assailant. The general consensus was of a man with a full beard, heavily tattooed, at least six foot three, probably taller. So much for eye-witnesses. They played up the fact that Allred had been the attorney hired by Edward Wrones, aka Fat Eddie, murdered so dramatically only four days earlier. Nobody from the department had tipped them about me, or at least they weren't publishing it yet. I handed the paper back to Phil.

"Kind of a bizarre story," I said.

His eyebrows went up. "Care to fill me in on any of the details?"

"Hey, haven't you heard? I don't talk to cops."

"Can't say as I blame you," he said, taking a sip of coffee through his straw. "How about giving me an opinion, then?"

"Glad to. You know what they say about opinions, though."

"Yeah. I'm curious, though. You think they'll ever catch this guy?"

"I turned it back on him. "You're in a better position to answer that than I am, now aren't you? What's your guess?"

"Hard to say. This guy's pretty cagey. He's careful. On the other hand, the brass really want him bad. The betting on the eighth floor right now is just about even money."

"Which side are you taking?"

"Me? I only bet on sure things, you know that."

"Yeah, I remember. How long is Volter going to have someone sitting out here baby-sitting me, anyway?"

"Probably forever." He let out the muffled wheeze that passes for a laugh with him. "I hear you gave Becker a little surprise welcome the other night."

"I didn't know it was him. It's just lucky I didn't blow his head off."

Phil wheezed again. "Lucky for who?" He didn't care much for Becker, either. He took another sip through the straw. "How's that lady friend of yours doing?"

"Fine. Just fine."

"Glad to hear it, Jason."

"Thanks," I said, and went back into the house.

For good or bad, I reflected, my life had changed radically. There was no way I could go back to work in the department, whether they proved anything or not. They'd never let me work again; they couldn't. They'd find some way to get rid of me.

Jennifer was still sitting in the kitchen. "What's going on, Jason?" she asked quietly.

I sat down and crossed my legs. "I don't really know what to say. I don't know how you're going to take this."

"Try me."

"You're not going to like it."

"Just tell me," she said.

I told her everything; what I had believed, Fat Eddie, Allred, Holzer, the killings, Dave

Warren on my track, everything. I watched her face carefully when I talked about the killings, but I couldn't get a reading. She listened carefully, head to one side, eyes scrunched up, focused on the table. It was the first time I'd been able to talk about it, to verbalize what I had done. It bothered me. I'd been carried along by my rage, but now, after it was all over, it made me feel very strange to be talking about it. I felt dislocated. Only a true psychotic can kill another human being without feeling something. I began to see how crazy it must appear to someone else.

When I finished, there was a long silence. Jennifer finally looked up at me. I half expected to see an expression of loathing on her face. Instead, there was an expression of thoughtful concern.

"Are they going to catch you?" she finally asked.

"I don't think so."

Her face showed relief, and she nodded slowly. "At least there's that. That's the important thing."

"I was afraid you might feel different about it."

"I don't know how I feel about it." She sighed. "I can't even think about it. It doesn't seem real to me. Nothing seems real, not that, not Brian, not anything."

"It is, though."

"I know. It just doesn't feel that way. At least it's over."

I hunched over in the chair, not quite knowing how to tell her, or even if I should. She looked at the expression on my face and gave me a searching look.

"It is over, Jason, isn't it?"

I looked down at the table.

"It *is* over, isn't it?" she repeated.

"No. Not quite."

"What do you mean, not quite?"

"Holzer. The biker. He's not going to let it rest."

"What do you mean? What is he going to do?"

"I don't have the slightest idea, but he's going to do something to get at me, you can bet on it."

She got up from the kitchen table and walked back and forth, looking upset. That wasn't too surprising.

"Can't you just leave?" she asked. "I mean, just leave Salt Lake? Go somewhere else?"

"Yeah, I can. I'm thinking about it." I took a deep breath. "I was hoping you'd come with me."

"Where?"

"Wherever. I thought maybe San Francisco. Your dance thing sort of went down the drain, but I'll bet you could get them to look at you again, given what happened. Arty people love high drama."

She smiled wryly. "True. Cynical, but true. At least it makes me stand out from the herd."

"No doubt about it," I agreed.

She stared off into space, considering. "I'll have to think about it, Jason. I don't know how I feel about anything right now."

"That's okay," I said. "I've got a few things to think about myself."

* * *

We didn't go out over the weekend. We talked a little, but Jennifer spent most of her time sitting and staring out the window, not saying much. I didn't push her. Phil Sandahl and Becker traded shifts watching the house.

Jennifer spent Monday morning on the phone. I spent it collecting my stuff and then typing out a short letter of resignation, "for personal reasons." Jennifer asked what I was doing so I handed her the letter.

"Funny, but I never even thought about that," she said, looking at it. "Of course. You can't just pick up and go back to work, can you?"

"No, I'm afraid not."

"You really want me along, Jason? I haven't been very good luck for you."

"I thought you had to think about things."

"I've thought about them."

I took the letter back from her and grabbed my stuff.

"I'll be back as soon as I turn this in," I told her. "Before you have a chance to change your mind."

I stopped to speak to Phil Sandahl before I got into my car. "Just heading downtown to administration," I said. "I'll wait for you in the parking lot if you get caught in traffic."

"That's what I like about you, Jase. Always a gentleman."

The more I thought about it, the more the idea of leaving town appealed to me. As long as I was in town, I was a target. If I disappeared long enough, maybe it would all just fade away. Holzer couldn't last too much longer.

He was too psycho. He was bound to self-destruct. The department wouldn't give up their investigation, but it would ease off a little if I wasn't right under their noses, a constant challenge. I didn't have any real attachment to Salt Lake. Leaving started to look good. Leaving with Jennifer started to look very good.

When I walked into the Metro Building it was weird. Fellow cops, guys I'd known for years, stopped dead when they saw me. Some walked away. Others nodded a polite and neutral greeting. Not one of them asked me what I was doing there. I went up to Marge Lesnick's office. Marge was the administrative secretary. There's one in every department, in every corporation. She was the one who knew how to do everything. She was the one who knew everything that was going on. If the chief didn't show up for a couple of weeks, things would run pretty much as usual. If Marge took two weeks off, the police department would grind to a halt.

I handed her the letter of resignation. She took it without comment. I turned in my badge, gun, and radio, along with the various other articles the department had issued me over the years; tape recorder, flak jacket, nightstick, etc. Marge checked them all off from my folder.

"Well, everything's here," she said, "except for a spare magazine."

Some years ago the department had experimented briefly with using Smith & Wesson 9 mm. automatics. They worked great, except the damn thing had a disconcerting habit of discharging if they were dropped, whether the safety was on or off. After a number of embarrassing incidents, it was decided to go back to revolvers. My automatic was long since turned in, but apparently I had forgotten to turn in the spare clip.

"I haven't the slightest idea where it is," I told her.

"You're going to have to pay for it then, Jason. It's still signed out to you." She looked up and must have seen the look on my face. "I'm sorry," she added defensively. "If it's not signed in, you have to pay for it. It's signed out to you."

"Sorry, Marge, I've got a few other things on my mind."

"I know," she said. She hesitated, then leaned over the desk toward me. "We're going to miss you, Jason. I wish none of this had happened."

"You and me both." I smiled at her. "Tell you what. Have the department send me a bill. As soon as I get it, I'll drop everything and rush right down here with a check."

"You don't have to get sarcastic," she said mildly.

I apologized and backed out of the office. Marge reminded me of my third grade teacher, and if I spent too long there, that's how I started acting. Old habits die hard.

I drove back home feeling a whole lot lighter. We would go to San Francisco, stay with Willard until we got settled. I didn't quite know what I was going to do there, but it didn't matter. I'd find something. And I'd have Jennifer.

She was a lot more cheerful by the time I got home. "I called some dance people in San Francisco," she said. "It looks like things might actually work out. Can you believe it? How soon can we leave?"

"Just as soon as we can get packed. Except there are a few things to settle here. Day after tomorrow, I guess."

She shook her head rapidly. "We ought to leave right now or tomorrow morning. I've got a bad feeling about staying here any longer, Jason. A real bad feeling."

"I know what you mean," I said, "but that's just nerves talking. It'll be okay." I gestured outside at Phil Sandahl. "Look. We've even got police protection."

"I guess. I just want to get out of here before something else happens."

"We will. Nothing else is going to happen."

"Promise?"

"Promise."

She brightened up. "You didn't keep the last one, you know."

"What?"

"Promise. You promised to take me to the zoo, remember? I still want to go."

"You feel well enough?"

"As a matter of fact, I do. I feel pretty good. And I really want to get out for a while. I just want to go somewhere nice and forget about all this."

Actually, it did sound nice. Animals are a great antidote to people. Hogle Zoo was right up by where I lived, anyway. I went into the bedroom, checked my Walther, and slipped it into my belt under my shirt, in the familiar place behind my right hip. I didn't want Jennifer to see it. It would remind her of unpleasant things. Technically, since I had just resigned, I couldn't carry a gun, but I wasn't about to step outside the house without one.

Twenty minutes later we were buying tickets at the front gate of the zoo. Phil Sandahl followed us there, but he didn't get out of his car. He settled down in the parking lot and gave me a mocking wave as we went by. His job was just to keep a record of where I went, not step right on my heels.

Hogle is a pretty nice zoo for a small city. It has all the up-to-date ideas: a large aviary you can walk through where the birds fly around free, wolves gliding in a penned-off field instead of a cage, and so on. I liked the wolves.

When I was a kid, maybe nine or ten, I used to go to the Museum of Natural History. There were glass-fronted displays set into the walls that they called dioramas, with all kinds of different stuffed animals. There was one in particular I remember, off in a side corridor. Two wolves, caught in midstride, loping across the snow. The back wall was a painting of a pine forest, with a frozen river in the distance. It blended together so well it seemed real, at least to a kid. The corridor was dark, and the only light was a dim bluish-gray illumination supposed to make it look like moonlight. I used to stand for hours, staring and dreaming, dreaming and wondering, until it became so compelling I could hear the far-off wolf howls, and the hoarse panting, and the crunch of snow beneath padded feet. I don't know why it fascinated me so, or what it meant to me, but it certainly meant something.

At the zoo, though, the most impressive animals are the big cats. They have them in regular cages, but the cats also have access to an outside enclosure. There they loll around on the rock shelves, separated from the visitors not by bars, but by a deep trench. From the path outside, the wall in front is only four feet high, and you can look straight across to where they lie, but there is a sloping rock incline that leads to the bottom of the pit, and from there it's about a twenty-five-foot leap to get out. I'm sure the people at the zoo know what they're doing, but every once in a while you can catch the tigers eyeing that leap with a speculative gleam.

The cats spend a lot of their time outside in the summer, not just for the sun, but to get away from the people banging on the bars. The children are the worst. They do everything possible to get a rise out of the cats, short of poking them with sticks through the bars, and I wouldn't put that past them either if they thought they could get away with it. Meanwhile, their proud parents beam fondly at the little monsters. The kids remind me of monkeys in the treetops, teasing the carnivores looking up hungrily from the ground below, safe in their lofty haven. Just once I'd like to see a cage door swing open, and see the expression as one of them metaphorically fell to earth. I guess I was still feeling a little cynical about the human race. A bumper sticker I had seen on the way to the zoo summed it all up for me. It read, "If they can send a man to the moon, why can't they send them all?"

We watched the big cats until almost closing time. The people thinned out until we were the only ones there. Mostly, we watched the tigers. They sprawled in the afternoon sun and watched us back. Lions may be the king of beasts, but it is the tiger that is lord of the jungle. The tigers looked bored, but as they gazed disdainfully at us, I swear I could see a flicker of hunger way back behind those yellow eyes.

I was just standing there musing, wondering what tigerish thoughts were passing through those tiger minds, when Jennifer grabbed my arm. I looked up, startled, and standing about twenty feet from us, right at a turn in the path, was good old Brian.

I eased my hand toward my hip and started to back away, pulling Jennifer with me. I didn't want to shoot him or grab him or have anything to do with him. I just wanted to get the hell out of there.

If it hadn't been for Brian, I don't think he could have gotten that close to us. I don't know where he came from. Jennifer was standing right next to me, but all my attention was focused on Brian. Holzer came up right behind us. I must have backed right into him, and before I knew what was happening, he had one arm around Jennifer's throat, and in his right hand was a very nasty-looking .357. The muzzle was pressed up against her temple. He held her close, like a shield. She stood motionless, frozen, not making a sound.

"Easy, Coulter," he said. "Toss your piece over here."

He cocked the hammer back with his thumb. The barrel of the gun didn't waver an inch. I slid the Walther out of my belt, slowly and carefully, and did what he said. He never took his eyes off me. He hadn't even noticed Brian. He thought we were alone. When he heard the clunk of the gun hitting the ground, he relaxed a little.

"Let her go," I said. "You've got what you want." He shook his head.

"No way, Coulter. You fucked with me. Nobody fucks with me. Now it's pay-back time. You're dead. But this is even better. She dies; you watch. Then you die."

There wasn't time to think or plan. I reacted on instinct, knowing he was about to pull the trigger. I dove to the side, hit the ground and rolled, reaching in my shirt, going for a non-existent weapon. If he thought I was going for a gun, maybe he would rush his shot a little. He reacted instinctively as well, firing at me as I came up. Everything shifted into slow motion. The sound of the shot was distant, almost muffled, a huge rumbling reverberation that echoed out in waves. I could see the muzzle flash from the gun, and how the barrel jerked up with the force of the recoil. I noted with complete detachment that he had missed. The barrel leveled off, and I could see the round opening under the front sight. It looked large enough to crawl into. He squeezed the trigger again, and I could see with hideous clarity the hammer draw back and the cylinder revolve. He wasn't going to miss again.

Then Jennifer was moving, reaching up toward his arm, grabbing just as he fired again. The bullet went wide, and she went down, stunned, as he hit her with his free hand. Out of the corner of my eye I saw a figure coming toward him. It was Brian, charging to the rescue. I don't know what was in his mind. Maybe he thought Jennifer was his alone to control. Maybe he had a moment of sanity, was actually trying to save her. Maybe he didn't know what he was doing.

He got to within five feet before Holzer fired. The bullet caught Brian right in the chest, and he staggered back from the impact, then sank to his knees and fell over on his side. He never made a sound. As soon as he fired, Holzer spun back toward me, but he was half a second slow. I hit him waist high, driving him back into the concrete wall. He knew he was going over and grabbed at me as he toppled. Grabbing and failing, we went over the wall together.

It was a long drop, a very long drop. I was on top when we hit the ground, but it still stunned me. I could feel the breath go out of him in a rush, and the gun he had been clutching like death went flying through the air and bounced off a wall. It took me about ten seconds to clear my head enough to stagger to my feet. I didn't think anything was broken, but my whole side hurt like hell.

Holzer hadn't been so lucky. He was still lying there, cursing with whatever breath he had left. He looked right at me and said, "My fuckin' ribs are broken. My leg is all fucked up." It was unreal. It was almost like he was asking for my sympathy.

I noticed that his .357 had ended up only about five feet from his right shoulder, and thought I'd better retrieve the gun before he started looking around for it. I took two steps toward him, and then stopped short. Ten feet above, on the incline leading down to the bottom of the pit, stood a very large, very interested cat. I paused, hardly breathing. The informative sign out front had proclaimed that the enclosure contained a pair of Siberian tigers, the male ten feet long from tip to tail, weighing in at over seven hundred pounds. He had seemed impressive enough lying lazily on his rock perch. There aren't any words in our language to describe what he looked like now. I glanced up at the wall out of the corner of my eye, careful not to even move my head. The wall was sheer, offering nothing.

Holzer was pawing at his leg, still cursing. He hadn't noticed the big male above him yet. He sat up with a grunt, and the cat tensed all over. He focused intently on Holzer, so I took a chance and started backing away slowly toward the other corner of the pit. The cat's eyes flickered briefly toward me, but he seemed more interested in the figure lying on the ground. Maybe it was because Holzer was obviously hurt. Or maybe I was just finally having a bit of luck.

The front wall was smooth and unbroken, but the walls on either side were mortared in a patchwork fashion to give the appearance of genuine stone instead of concrete. There were irregular cracks and edges running all the way to the top. It was just conceivable that, using the corner as a brace, I could climb it. I'd climbed similar rock faces before, up in Little Cottonwood, though never with quite so much at stake. The hardest thing was getting my hands to stop sweating long enough to get a grip. Fear is bad company for a climber.

By this time Holzer had finally looked up and noticed the tiger. "Jesus, fuck," he mouthed, barely audible. The cat's ears twitched. He was stalking Holzer playfully, one slow padded step at a time. He probably hadn't had this much fun in years. His mate was still high on the ledge, watching with great interest, sitting up now.

Holzer just might have been all right if he had simply closed his eyes and lain there without moving. Zoo animals in general, and cats in particular, are unpredictable. The tiger might have attacked him, or he might have left him alone. But Holzer couldn't do it, just lie there. His nerve wouldn't hold. He started looking around frantically, and his eyes found the gun. He scuttled over to it clumsily, one leg dragging, and snatched it off the ground. As soon as he moved, of course, the cat was on him. Holzer desperately brought the revolver up and fired a round right into the middle of the striped head bearing down on him.

A round from a .357 magnum at close range will tear the top right off a person's head, scattering bone and ripping apart the soft gray matter inside. A tiger's head is constructed somewhat differently. A large shelf of thick and solid bone sits over the eyes, protecting its furry, feline thoughts. A rifle will penetrate that shelf. A .44 magnum handgun might, if the angle is right. A .357 will not.

The bullet hit the cat square between his ears, coming in at a slight angle, and ricocheted off with a dull whine. The effect on the tiger was about the same as if someone were to hit you right between the eyes with a fist. It surprised the animal. It stunned him a moment. It threw him back on his haunches. It hurt him, probably a lot. And it made him very, very angry.

A quick bound, and he had Holzer in his jaws, tearing at him. Holzer screamed, a high-pitched shriek of atavistic horror, the shriek of the primate finally caught by the predator he had teased so often. He tried to shoot again, but the gun dropped from fingers suddenly useless at the end of a clawed and tattered arm. Holzer squirmed on the ground, still trying somehow to fend the tiger off. I had a quick vision of Stony carrying the jay across the street. But Holzer couldn't fly, and there was nowhere for him to go. The cat kept at him, and then his mate came bounding down the rock to get in on the action. She grabbed one shoulder and started dragging Holzer back up toward the rock ledge, but the male refused to let go. After a couple of violent shakes of her head Holzer's shoulder finally gave, and his arm simply separated from his body. He was still screaming. It seemed to go on forever. Finally the male got a firm grip on his head with his jaws and gave a sharp twist. There was a crunching sound audible even over Holzer's screams. The screams abruptly stopped.

I had been watching, paralyzed, until I realized it wouldn't be long before one of those cats remembered there was another morsel in the other corner of the pit. I turned and faced the wall. I tried to put everything out of my mind, just viewing the wall as a climbing problem. I hooked my fingers in the first crack and pulled myself up. Then one foot, one set of toes precariously braced. Then a hand, searching for another hold. I didn't look down to see what the cats were doing.

Everything was going fine until about three-quarters of the way up. My foot slipped, leaving me hanging for a moment by my fingers. The motion almost undid me, since it attracted the notice of the big male. I heard a sort of coughing grunt, and the sound of soft pads thumping on the concrete floor below. I looked over my shoulder. I shouldn't have, but I couldn't help it. The tiger gathered himself and made a tremendous spring up toward me. He almost got me, too. Six inches higher and he would have hooked me by one dangling ankle and peeled me off that wall.

I resisted the urge to scramble up the wall more quickly toward the safety of the path. Slow and deliberate. Easy does it. Fingers and toes. Hug the wall. The tiger didn't even try again. I guess he wasn't used to so much action all at once.

I made it over the wall and collapsed on the path, almost caressing the solid ground. Jennifer grabbed me, her face ashen, still stunned by Holzer's blow. She tried to ask me something, probably if I was all right, but not much was coming out. I wasn't doing a lot better myself.

I pulled myself together, made it to my feet, and stumbled over to where Brian was lying. He hadn't moved. I put my fingers on his carotid, just out of habit, but I didn't expect to feel anything, and I didn't.

"Is he dead?" Jennifer asked, almost in a whisper.

I nodded. "We need to get out of here."

I scooped up the Walther, which was still lying where I had dropped it, and pulled Jennifer away. We made our way toward the exit. We had our arms around each other, but I don't know who was supporting whom. Halfway down the path, I heard a scream. Someone, finally attracted by the shots and commotion, had discovered the scene. We kept on going.

Near the exit, zoo personnel came running past, desperation on their faces. Two steps behind them came Phil Sandahl, breathing hard. He stopped when he saw me and put his hand on his holster, but didn't draw his gun.

"I heard shots," he panted. It was a long way from the parking lot. "What the fuck have you done now?"

"Not me. Some guy fell in the tiger pit and tried to shoot his way out."

He stared at me, mouth working. "You son of a bitch. You son of a bitch. Volter is going to kill me." He hesitated, torn between going on to see what had happened and keeping me in sight.

"Go ahead, Phil," I said, gesturing up the path. "I'm just going back home. You can find me there. Really." He stood irresolute, until another scream decided him.

"Son of a bitch," he repeated, almost snarling, and sprinted toward the noise.

Jennifer spent the entire ride home staring out the window, hands clenching and unclenching. There wasn't anything I could say, so I didn't say anything. I finally spoke as we pulled up in front of the house.

"Well," I said, "at least there's one thing. It really *is* over now."

"I can't deal with this," she said.

"You don't do so bad. You saved my life you know. When you grabbed his arm. You weren't in such good shape, yourself."

She ignored me. "I just can't deal with this."

I couldn't think of anything more to say. I parked the car, and we went inside the house.

SIXTEEN

Three days later we were ready to leave. The stuff I really wanted, which wasn't a lot, was snugged away in a storage locker. Everything else could just be left behind. We were going to take two cars, hers and mine. It took some doing to get Jennifer's bug out of the impound evidence lot, but since all the suspects in her abduction were dead anyway, they finally agreed to release it.

Stony didn't like what was happening, all the packing and moving. He kept prowling around, giving occasional yowls. He wasn't quite sure what was going on, but he knew he didn't like it.

There was something I didn't like, either. Nobody from the department showed up to talk to me. The surveillance outside the house had been pulled. I called a few people downtown, cops I thought might talk to me, just trying to get a reading, but if anyone knew anything they weren't saying. True, Volter knew I wasn't going to be talking, and except for the fact I had been at the zoo, there wasn't any hard evidence to connect me up to what had happened there. I tried to convince myself that Volter had simply given up on it temporarily, but I didn't really buy that.

Jennifer was quiet. She wanted to leave Salt Lake and wipe out every memory of the past week. I was just glad to be an exception to that. She still didn't much want to talk about what had happened to her, and I didn't press it. I was curious how Brian had talked her into meeting him that night in City Creek Canyon, though, and finally she brought it up.

Brian had called her at the studio that day and apologized abjectly for the way he had been acting. He told her he was leaving town and wanted to see her one last time, just to make things okay. "He was like the Brian of old," she said, shaking her head ruefully. She agreed to meet him up in City Creek, at the place where they used to picnic when they first met. Just to wrap it up, he said, the old place, the beginning and the ending. Only, his idea of a suitable ending was a permanent one.

It was difficult enough for us to start talking again, but there was another thing that really had me worried, and that was making love. I didn't know when to do it, or how, or even if. For the next two days nothing was said on either side. We slept in the same bed, we made plans for the future, we finally talked at length about what had happened, both to her and to me. We managed to get back some of the ease that had made things so special. We even laughed together a couple of times. But that was all. The third night I reached for her, cautiously, hesitantly, and she came to me slowly. We held each other, both nervous, both awkward. I didn't think it was going to work. After a few tentative kisses she pulled away and wrapped the sheet tight around her shoulders.

"You okay?" I asked.

"I think so. I was just thinking, it's not fair." I reached out and stroked her hair gently.

"No, it isn't," I said.

She turned on her side and propped herself up on one elbow, looking sadly at me. "Jason, do you want to make love?"

"Very much. Do you?"

"Very much. But I'm afraid. Not afraid of you, not afraid of making love. Afraid that I'll feel different about it. Afraid that you'll be different. Afraid that things won't be the same."

"Things never stay the same."

"That's something completely different."

"I know. I'm just talking."

"My God," she said, "it's hard enough to get through the awkwardness of the first time without having to go through this all over again." She made a face of such total annoyance and disgust that I had to laugh.

"Are you laughing at me, Jason?"

"Of course."

"Uncaring callous beast."

"Never uncaring."

Then she started laughing, and I started

laughing, and it was all right, and we made love, and it was good.

But that night I had a dream. It was strange, because I hadn't dreamed a thing all the time before that. I dreamed Jennifer was back. It had all been a terrible mistake. It was another girl who had been kidnapped, someone we all thought was Jennifer, but it wasn't. She was lying in bed with me, and we were talking about it, and then we started making love. I reached for her eagerly. She came to me slowly, stiffly, oddly reticent. I ran my hand over her stomach and down between her legs. She was cold there, cold as death. I withdrew my hand, disturbed, and started kissing her. Her tongue was warm and yielding, sweet. But there was something wrong there too. Her mouth became too sweet, overpowering, cloying, sticky, sugary and soft. Her tongue fell apart in my mouth, dissolving, souring, tasting like rancid, melted taffy.

I woke up with the taste still in my mouth. I had to get out of bed and get a drink of cold water. Jennifer didn't wake up, thank God. I didn't understand it. Last week, sure, when I thought she was dead. Not now. Anxiety, I told myself. Just fears, repressed fears. It was nothing to get disturbed about. It took me a very long time to get back to sleep.

In the morning I got the last of the stuff stowed away, and I was trying to entice Stony out from under the stove so I could pop him in a cat carrier, when I heard a car pull up in front of the house. I broke off the cat conversation and watched as Dave Warren got out of his car and walked slowly up to the house. I didn't like the look on his face. He stopped on the doorstep and spoke through the screen door. "Can I come in, Jase?"

I swung open the screen and held it as he walked by. He pulled up one of the hard-backed kitchen chairs that was left, turned it around back to front, and straddled it.

"Looks like you're about ready to leave," he said, looking around.

"Just about."

"Where to?"

"San Francisco."

He turned to Jennifer. "You going with him?"

She nodded. Dave tipped the chair back and balanced on the two back legs.

"You know, it's funny," he said slowly, "but I feel sort of responsible for this mess. If I hadn't got you two together, none of this would have happened. We'd still be working together, Jason, tracking down the case, and nobody would be dead."

"Except for me," Jennifer put in quietly. "I'd be dead."

"You did good, Dave," I added. "I know you don't think so, but you did good."

"Yeah, maybe." He rocked the chair farther back on its legs. "Maybe. Anyway, Jase, I thought you might like to hear about the follow-up at the zoo."

He looked at me expectantly, so I spread my hands in a gesture for him to continue.

"The gun that shot Brian Flannery was Holzer's," he said. I realized that I had never known Brian's last name.

"Interesting thing, we did a ballistics check

on it. It's the gun that killed that girl on State Street, the one who started this whole thing. Also that girl the county dicks found, Cynthia what's-her-name. Also—''

''I get the idea,'' I interrupted.

''Sure. Anyway, that was the gun that shot Brian. No question about it. But what I want to know is how did Holzer end up in the tiger cage?''

''Maybe he tripped.''

''Oh, he tripped all right, but he had some help. Want to know how I think it went down?'' Dave didn't wait for an answer. ''I think Holzer went into the pit before Brian was ever shot. I think you took his gun away, threw him over the wall, and then shot Brian with Holzer's gun and tossed it over the wall. That's what I think happened.''

''And who shot the tiger?''

Dave gave me a nasty grin. ''So you were there, Jase? Right at the scene?''

I had walked into that one. It just goes to show how easy it is to say something you don't mean to, no matter how smart you think you are. Luckily, it didn't really matter this time. There wasn't any case. Dave waited a moment, and when I didn't reply, went on.

''What I really can't figure is how you got the two of them there at the same time. Now that shows real inventive planning.''

For the first time, I heard coldness in his voice. His eyes looked at me as though I were total scum, the way he looked at people like Holzer and Fat Eddie. It stung me into replying.

''It wasn't that way, Dave, believe me.''

"Oh? Then how was it?" he challenged.

"Leave him alone, Dave," said Jennifer. "They followed us somehow. Jason didn't even know they were there."

"Jennifer," I said, warning her.

"What?" she said. "You didn't want it to happen that way." Dave just sat there, hoping for an argument to develop.

"Tell you what," I said. "How about if I tell you a hypothetical story, how I think something like that might have gone down."

"You do that," he said. "I'm all ears."

I ran down what had happened at the zoo for him as he rocked back and forth in the chair. I told it straight, just like it happened. He stared down at the floor the whole time, head bowed over the back of the chair. When he straightened up, that cold look was gone. It was just Dave and me, talking again.

"It fits," he said. "I couldn't understand it. The others I understood, but this was different. There wasn't any reason for it."

"There wasn't any reason for any of this, when you come right down to it."

"I was wondering when you'd figure that out." He looked grim suddenly. "I'm still working on the Allred case, you know."

"I didn't think you'd just give up. You never have."

"I went down to Allred's office yesterday afternoon for a last look before we unsealed it. The lab boys went through it pretty good, but I wanted to see it one last time."

"And?"

"And I was leaning against the desk, just thinking. The sun was shining in the window and it lit up the back of his chair, you know, that black vinyl cushion job he had?"

"Yeah," I said. There wasn't any point to claiming I'd never seen it, not to Dave. Besides, he was leading up to something. He wasn't really listening to me.

"On the back of the chair, just under the little nap on top, there was a little smear of dried blood. Allred's blood, I'd guess. I don't know how the lab guys missed it."

I had a sudden memory of absently wiping blood off my hand. Dave continued, not looking at me.

"Well, I stared at it for about an hour, and the long and short of it was I lifted a print off that chair."

He reached in his jacket pocket and took out a small evidence envelope. He squeezed it open and shook out a hinged fingerprint lift. I could see the ridged pattern of what looked like a pretty good thumbprint against the background. Jennifer looked at it curiously, disturbed, but not fully appreciating its significance. Dave put the lift on top of a nearby box, where it squatted like a malignant spider.

"Sooner or later, Jase, they all slip up."

"That's what you always told me, Dave."

"What's going on?" Jennifer asked, suddenly very scared.

"Just talking shop," I said. Dave seemed to be waiting for me to say something more.

"It's too bad you're so goddamn thorough," I said. "But you do good work."

"That was always your trouble, Jase. Too impulsive. Too quick. No respect for procedures. Guys like you should never be cops."

"No argument there."

Dave and I looked at each other over the back of the chair. A warbler trilled a little run outside the open window. I thought I'd never heard anything so ineffably sweet. The only other sound in the room was the creaking of the chair as Dave rocked back and forth. A fine and lazy summer's day.

After about ten years Dave glanced down at his watch, stood up, and stretched himself. He didn't look down at the fingerprint lift.

"Well," he said, "I'm late for an appointment, and I've got a shitload of work to do, and I don't have another partner yet to help me with it."

He smiled over at Jennifer. "You take care of him, now. He can't take care of himself, you know."

"I know," she said.

"You take care too, Jason."

"You too. It's a jungle out there."

"So I hear. So I hear."

He hesitated, started to hold out his hand, and then changed it into a little wave as he went out the door. I watched until his car turned the corner. Jennifer was standing by the chair, holding the lift in her hand, examining it curiously.

"What was all that about?" she asked. "What exactly is this, anyway?"

"A souvenir," I said thoughtfully. "Just a souvenir."

I reached down and took it from her hand. I started to tear it up, and then for some reason slipped it into my pocket. Jennifer was looking at me a little oddly.

"It's all okay then, Jason?"

"Yes," I said. "It's all okay." I looked around at the room. I'd spent a lot of my life in this house, but I didn't feel bad about leaving. It was time to start a new life. "Now if I can just get Stony out from under the stove, we can be on our way."

I walked into the kitchen and squatted down in front of the stove. Jennifer followed me in and put her hand on my shoulder. I could feel a tenseness in her arm.

"Hey, are you all right?" I asked.

She didn't answer for a moment. "Jason," she said, "you're not going to like this."

I knew what she was going to say before she said it. I guess I had known it really for the last couple of days.

"I can't go with you, Jason. I can't. I thought I could, but I can't."

I tried to say something, but she held up a hand and stopped me. Her eyes were focused on my face, but she wasn't looking at me.

"It's not fair," she said. "I know it's not fair. You took me in when I needed help. You saved my life. You gave up everything you had for me. I know what you've done for me, and what it's done to you. I do know.

"But every time I look at you now, I don't just see you, don't just see your face. What I see is death. It's not your fault, Jason; it isn't anybody's fault. It's just what happened. I do love you, I swear I do. But that doesn't seem to matter. I just can't go with you."

An anguished protest rose up and died in my throat. I guess I should have argued. Maybe that's what she expected, what she wanted, just some reassurance. Sometimes I lie awake and wonder about that. But it didn't matter. Like Jennifer, I just couldn't do it. I couldn't say anything, even though there were a thousand things that needed to be said. It seemed so perfectly logical, so absolutely right for me to lose her, after all. Punishing myself for my sins? Who knows.

"Where will you go?" was all I finally said.

"Portland, for a while. I've got a sister there. I don't like her much, but she's family."

"Drop me a postcard, will you?"

She came into my arms. It was the only time I'd seen her cry, and she let go, sobbing with all her heart. I held her close to me. There were tears starting in the back of my own eyes. We stood there clutching each other like drowning children, until it passed and we both stood back away at the same time. We always did have good timing.

Jennifer picked up her last piece of luggage, a little overnight bag, and went out the door without another word. I followed her out and sat down on the front step. Her VW *put-putted* away down the street. She didn't look back. She stopped at the corner and sat there for long enough to make me think she might have changed her mind, but then turned the corner and was gone. The old duffer across the street came out of his house, saw me sitting there, and waved a friendly hand. I waved back. Why not?

I looked at my car, all packed, and sat there feeling sorry for myself. All dressed up and nowhere to go. I got up and went back into the house. As I walked into the kitchen, Stony wormed his way out from his haven under the stove. I reached down to ruffle his head and he bounded out the window, adroitly avoiding my hand. I stared out the window after him. Cats, I thought. Maybe I should get myself a dog.

ABOUT THE AUTHOR

J.R. Levitt served as an officer on the Salt
Lake City Police Force for seven years. He
now lives in Alta, Utah, where he runs the
family ski lodge and is at work on his second
Jason Coulter mystery.

DEADLY DEALINGS

☐ **BINO by A.W. Gray.** Bino, is a white-haired, longhorn lawyer with the inside scoop on everything from hookers to Dallas high society. When his seediest client turns up dead, Bino suspects a whitewash of the dirtiest kind and goes on the offensive. What he finds links his client's demise to a political assassination, and the bodies start piling up. Politics has always been the dirtiest game in town—and it's about to become the deadliest.   (401298—$3.95)

☐ **FAVOR by Parnell Hall.** The third Stanley Hastings mystery brings the ambulance chaser-turned-private-detective to the seedy backroom poker games and glittery casinos of Atlantic City as a favor—a favor that will get Stanley indicted for grand larceny and named the prime suspect in two murders.   (401611—$3.95)

☐ **A CLUBBABLE WOMAN by Reginald Hill.** Sam Connon stood pale-faced and trembling in the darkened hall of his house, the telephone in his hand. Behind him, in the living room was his wife. She was quite, quite dead. And as even a distraught husband could tell, she must have known her killer very, very well. . . .   (155165—$3.50)

Prices slightly higher in Canada

Buy them at your local

bookstore or use coupon

on next page for ordering.